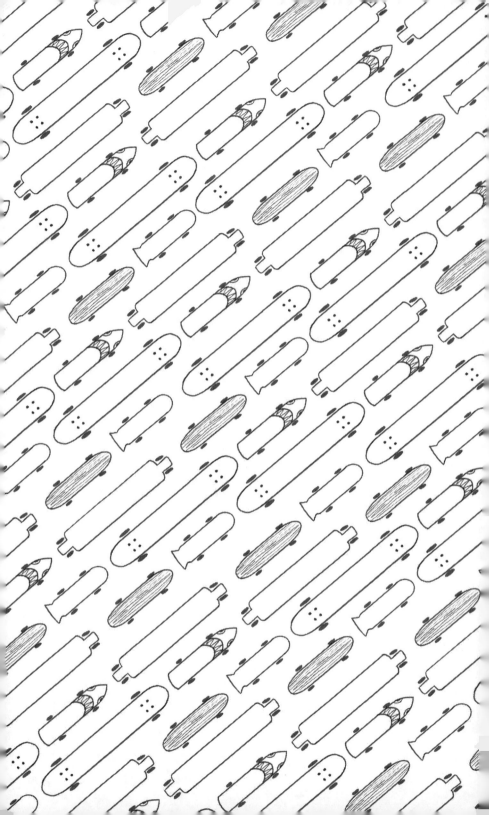

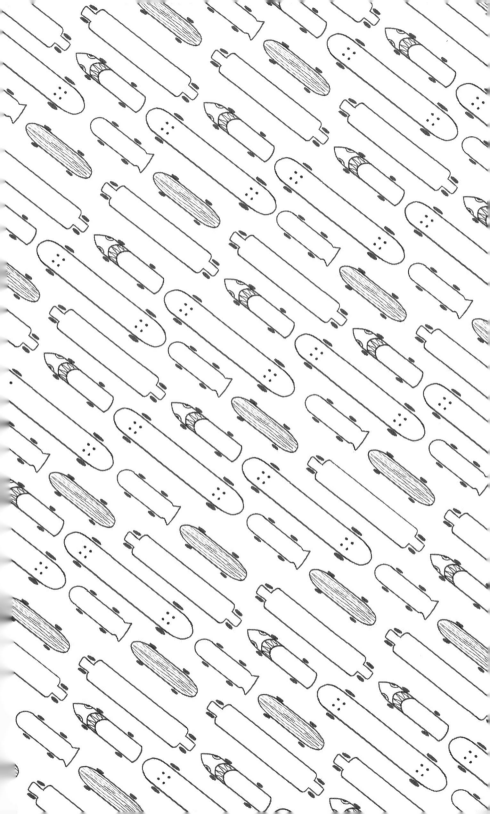

This Book Belongs To:

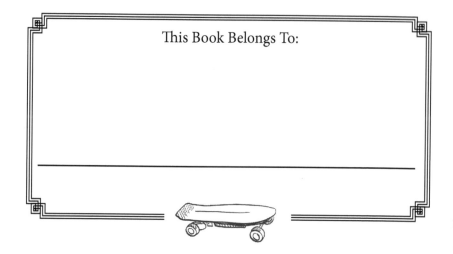

For additional information visit: HouseOfRoses.org

For permission from the publisher or information about special discounts available for bulk purchases, sales promotions or fund-raising and educational needs, please contact John V. Roselli at:

-Mr.RosesEmail@Gmail.com

Published in the USA, NY

ISBN#: 978-0-9995676-4-7

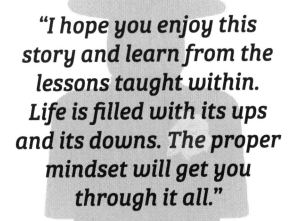

"I hope you enjoy this story and learn from the lessons taught within. Life is filled with its ups and its downs. The proper mindset will get you through it all."

- Mr. Roses

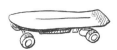

# Table of Contents

# BONEZ

## By: Mr. Roses

### Illustrated by: Amber Leigh Luecke

Bonez by: Mr. Roses

# CHAPTER 1 - THE INTRO

We open up the story with Quigz in a laughter. Then a slap to his back from Essie right after.

Quigz – Hey, what was that for? I'm just trying to get Bonez to man up. He just needs to be smooth and be like, hey Peep what's up.

Essie – Yeah, just like you did the other day? I remember seeing Sally and the Goonsquad forcing you to pay.

Quigz – It was a few old wristbands, nothing too special. Sally and the Goonsquad just like to play wrestle.

Essie – Looked more like a beatdown if you had to ask me.

And this was the crew, Quigz, Essie and Bonez; they were the three.

Quigz was a bit of a wild card, he always had something to say. His shirt was loose, his pants were tight, and they were always the color gray. His hair was long, red, and curly; his skateboard was a bright green. He was always doing wild things and creating an interesting scene.

Essie was the cool guy; at times it would go to his head. But a genuine heart and smart as a whip, he always made sure to be well-read. His hair was short and black; he always made sure to keep it in style. And he always seemed to get what he wanted, by showing off his smile.

Bonez is the good guy, always helping others and focusing on his dream. He wanted to be the best skater around, so he practiced every day with his team. Bonez is his given nickname; Gus was his original birth name. He loved his shirt with the skeleton boy, and from there his nickname came.

Bonez – Alright guys, enough. No need to get rough. With all this smack talk, are you ready to race? Andrews Street's pretty fast; it moves at a quick pace.

Downhill skateboarding is the sport of Letitbe's town. Sally with her huge skateboard, is the best skater around. But this was the year that Bonez would put Sally to the test. He's been practicing every day; he hasn't taken a day's rest. Tomorrow was the big race, that's always close to the end of summer. Bonez believes he can beat Sally and take the title from her.

*"Follow your dreams, follow your heart.*

*Anything is achievable if you work hard and play your part."*

# Chapter 1 - The Intro

# CHAPTER 2 - THE RACE TO THE ICE CREAM SHOP

Bonez – Alright guys, on three, let's race to the ice cream shop.

Essie – Get ready Quigz, remember the last time, your flop?

Quigz – Don't worry about me—just focus on yourself.

Essie – I can only focus on those pants; they make you look like an elf.

The boys set off, heading down the block. Right as they started, Quigz slipped on a rock. A tumble, a roll, then back on his feet. And the three boys were off, racing down the street.

Out of the three, Bonez was the best. Anyone who's seen him skate was always impressed.

Bonez rode a little yellow banana board. On it he would move with great speed. Always a desire to keep going faster, was something he seemed to need.

Not only did Bonez skate fast, he did it with some style. He could even skate on just two wheels and do that for about a mile.

Continuing down the hill, the three boys headed towards a loop. After the turn and right up ahead stood a familiar group.

Essie – Hey, Quigz, check it out. It's Sally and her crew.

Quigz – Sweet. Check this out guys; get a good view.

Sally, always dressed in yellow, she is pretty and tough as could be. She rolled with the toughest skaters in town: Goon one, Goon two, and Goon three.

Sally and Quigz always seemed to be at war. She beats him up, then Quigz messes with her some more.

Quigz skated over towards Sally, right at her and the tough Goonsquad. Quigz looked in Sally's eyes and smiled, then hit her with a nod.

In the street, next to the sidewalk, was a puddle right where they stood. Quigz yelled 'Shower time!' as he skated through the puddle and soaked them all real good.

Quigz – Make sure to add some soap and clean behind your ears!

Quigz yelled as he kept skating along. Essie and Bonez were laughing in tears.

The boys kept on skating; they were moving—practically flying down the street. Now they were approaching a group of girls that Essie always wanted to meet.

Essie – Hey check this out guys. It's time to impress. I'll hit them with a power slide, for the ladies nothing less.

Crouching down low, Essie pivoted and started sliding sideways down the street. Moving fast, he slid past the girls and held it for a few feet. The girls seemed to be entertained by Essie and his style. And of course they turned red, when Essie looked back and hit them with his smile.

Towards the bottom of the hill, the boys headed with great speed. Up in front was Bonez, he's always in the lead.

The ice cream shop was close, it was on the corner at the end of Andrews street. And there she was, standing out front, it was time for her and Bonez to meet.

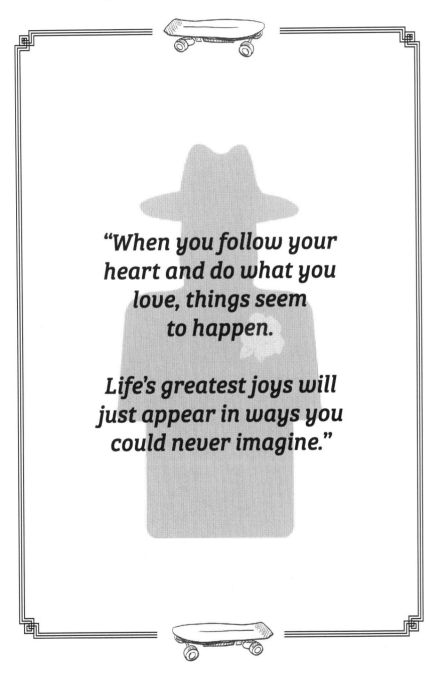

*"When you follow your heart and do what you love, things seem to happen.*

*Life's greatest joys will just appear in ways you could never imagine."*

# Chapter 3 - Bonez Meets Peep

With tremendous speed, the boys headed towards the ice cream shop.

Quigz – I'm bailing boys. I'm not sure if I can stop!

Essie – I'm right with you. Let's hop on the grass over there!

But Bonez kept on going; their fears he didn't share.

Bonez made it to the bottom. He raised his arms high up in the air. He slowed himself down, then looked back at the boys while rolling without a care.

Bonez – I did it, I did it!

Then something quick caught his eye. He was about to crash into a girl who was out front innocently standing by. He couldn't stop himself and unfortunately had to bail. Embarrassed by the fall he took, Bonez's face quickly started to turn pale.

Peep – Hey are you alright? I didn't mean to get in your way!

Bonez got up quickly but didn't know what to say.

Bonez – Ugh yeah, I'm alright. I didn't mean to get you scared.

Peep – It's alright, I heard you coming. I was a little prepared.

Bonez – Well anyways, I'm Bonez. It's nice to meet you.

Peep – Hi, I'm Peep. It's nice to meet you too.

Peep was the girl that Bonez always wanted to meet. A quiet girl with an innocent face, who seemed very sweet.

Peep dressed in bright colors, like a hippie some would say. Her hair was brown, her shape was small, and her eyes were a light bluish-gray.

For a moment, Bonez and Peep stood there; not a single word was said. Then a blush came over and appeared on Peep; her face quickly then turned red.

Bonez – By chance, tomorrow, do you have any plans? I have a big race and could really use some fans. It's a race to the bottom from Kent down to Seaview.

Peep – I'm free tomorrow, and I'll bring a friend—we'll come and support you!

Peep started off talking, saying many things quite fast. In and out of Bonez's ears, many words then had passed. Bonez stood there and listened but was lost in a daze. The words passed through his head, each phrase came in a phase.

As Bonez stood there blankly, he tried to connect the dots. He thought of the words that Peep was saying and filled in some of the spots: 'First it was something about her friend taking photos of me. Then something about her friend's friends, not sure what that could be. Then something about tomorrow and how it's going to be nice.'

Then there was a loud yell in Sally's voice, 'Quigz, you're going to pay the price!'

Right at that moment, Bonez snapped out of his daze.

Sally – You're going to pay Quigz, and I can think of a few different ways!

Sally walked over to Quigz, he was leaning on a short wood fence. The Goonsquad picked him up by the ankles, and out fell a few cents. The crew was still wet from the splash and all full of anger. It seemed like Quigz, was yet again, heading towards some danger.

All dressed in black leather, the Goonsquad was made up of three big brothers. The toughest skaters in all of the town, was how they were described by others. They rolled with Sally, and she was just as tough as the three. You didn't want to mess with this crew; that anyone would agree.

Sally then grabbed Quigz and spun him right around. She lifted him from under his arms and again Quigz was off the ground.

Peep then stopped talking, her and Bonez looked at Sally holding Quigz in the air.

Quigz – I love it when you hold me Sally; it shows that you really care.

Bonez – Ugh. Hey Peep, it was nice talking but I think I have to run. I hope to see you tomorrow; the race should be some fun.

Sally and the Goonsquad left as Bonez was heading over towards Essie and Quigz. Sally dropped Quigz over the fence, in the mud to hang with the pigs. As the boys helped Quigz out of the mud, Bonez looked back at Peep, embarrassed but with a smile. Peep smiled back as she looked at Bonez, and that lasted a long while.

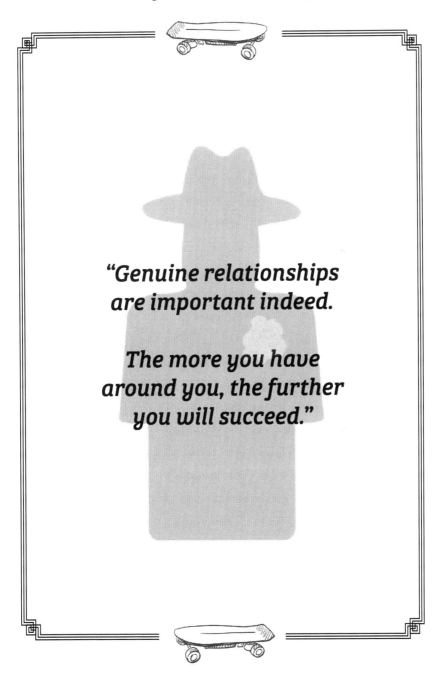

*"Genuine relationships are important indeed.*

*The more you have around you, the further you will succeed."*

# CHAPTER 4 – AT THE TOP OF KENT STREET

Today was the day that Bonez had been prepping for: a race down Kent Street, to the bottom by the shore. It was the quickest hill in all of Letitbe's town. The view at the top was the best around. The ocean, the cliffs, and the comfortable breeze. A feeling of calm the view always guarantees.

Essie – Are you nervous, Bonez? You're standing quite still.

Bonez – No, I'm alright; just have a little chill.

Essie – It's just some nerves. I wouldn't worry too much. You're the best skater around. You have the magic touch.

It was a beautiful day, not a cloud in the sky. To watch the race, people from all over came by. There was a group of people, forming at the top of the hill. Every spot that was open now started to fill.

Quigz – Gents, I'm excited. Today's going to be great! Bonez you'll beat Sally; I know that's something she's going to hate. I could just see it now and imagine the things that will be said.

Essie – Alright, Quigz. Enough. Don't get in Bonez's head.

Bonez – No. it's alright. I have to psych myself out.

Essie – Bonez, you're going to beat her; there's absolutely no doubt.

Bonez was confident but there was something on his mind. There was a face in the crowd that he couldn't seem to find. With all the excitement that was going on around, Peep's bright smile was nowhere to be found.

It was now getting closer to the start of the race. There was excitement and joy on everyone's face. Sally and the Goonsquad had finally arrived and a feeling of butterflies Bonez now felt inside.

Sally – Ah, I'm excited; this is going to be great. Let's see what you can do, Bonez. Let's see how you skate.

Laughing at Bonez's skateboard, saying how it was like hers but just so small. Bonez didn't care what Sally said; he didn't listen to her at all.

Quigz – I wouldn't be so excited, Sally, if I were you.

Sally – You shouldn't be talking, Quigz, unless it's a fight you're trying to get into.

Bonez stood there silent, trying to get in the zone. He imagined no one was around him; he imagined he was alone. But there was just one thought that he couldn't get out of his mind. Then he heard 'Say cheese!' coming from behind.

Peep stood there with her friend; her friend had a camera in hand.

Peep – Smile, Bonez, let's see them teeth, don't just awkwardly stand!

A smile came over Bonez. He smiled from ear to ear. Then all the nerves that Bonez was feeling suddenly seemed to disappear.

From Kent Street down to Seaview, that was the name of the beach. On the mic, the announcer tapped, and then began his speech.

Announcer – Alright, all you people, are you ready for a nice show? I'll do a countdown on the mic, and then the skaters will go!

*"Nerves will come, nerves will go.*

*When nerves appear, calm yourself down and take it slow."*

24

# Chapter 4 - At the Top of Kent Street

# CHAPTER 5 – THE RACE TO SEAVIEW

Bonez stood at the starting line. Sally lined up and looked over at him.

Announcer – Alright skaters, three-two-one, now let the race begin!

The announcer at that point sounded a bell. At the same time, the whole crowd started to yell. Sally and Bonez each took off, both with great speed. Side by side and very close together, it was hard to tell who had the lead.

Kent Street's design was shaped like an S. Steep and curvy, it was something you had to finesse. Right down the middle was a set of stairs. The crowd ran down them and did so with cheers.

Around the first bend was a close one indeed. Sally bumped into Bonez; almost falling, he lost a bit of speed. Flustered but focused, Bonez kept on straight ahead. As they approached the stairs landing, Sally now led.

Sally – Oops, watch out, next time you might just get pushed off the road!

She yelled back at Bonez, her strength and toughness she always showed.

Sally then slipped by the stairs landing and almost fell to the ground. The sand from the beach, the wind picks up and moves it all around. Sally regained her balance and continued on with the race. Bonez slipped but kept on moving forward, determination was written all over his face.

As Bonez passed the stairs landing, he started kicking off the street to give him more speed. As they approached the next turn, Bonez was gaining on Sally and slowly closing in on her lead.

As Sally began her turn, Bonez cut in tight right on the inside of the road. He popped a wheelie as he skated past Sally—full of anger, she was about to explode.

Feverishly, Sally started kicking; she was steaming, you could see it coming out of her ears. The end of the race, the skaters were approaching. The crowd was watching, now bursting in cheers.

At this point, both of the skaters, they were kicking off the ground, giving it everything they got. The crowd was filling around the finish line; they were taking up the whole lot.

Kent Street led into a parking lot for the beach we know as Seaview. From lamppost to the stair railing was the finish line that the skaters had to skate through.

Neck and neck, the skaters approached the finish line. Both crouching low as they went down the last incline.

Passing the finish line together, both skaters were moving quick. Stunned in silence, the crowd all stood there, all you heard was a single...

'Click.'

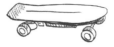

*"Throughout life challenges are always bound to appear.*

*Face them all head on. Afterwards, their lessons will be clear."*

# Chapter 5 - The Race to Seaview

# CHAPTER 6 - THE DECISION

Announcer – Wow, folks, I'm not sure how to call this one! Out of all that I've hosted, this was the closest run!

While everyone stood silent, Sally started chanting that she won the race. Then a short brunette girl stepped out from the crowd and said, 'No that's not the case.' This pretty brunette girl walked straight to the announcer with confidence all over her face.

Bree – Excuse me, sir, I have a photo. It is Bonez who has won the race. Both skaters extended their arm and fingers, look here, my photo shows it all. The first to pass the finish line wins, you must treat it like touching an imaginary wall.

The announcer examined the photo and could see it clear as day.

Announcer – Just by a fingertip, he passed it first! Bonez is our new champ today!

Stunned, Bonez stood there; he was always a modest sort of boy. The energy around him, as everyone cheered, was something he seemed to enjoy.

For the next few minutes, the parking lot was quite a scene. There was music playing, people dancing, and everything in between. There was action going on everywhere and it was all due to Bonez's exciting win. All the energy floating in the air, Bonez could feel it in his skin.

Essie – Bonez! You did it! I knew it, man!

Quigz – I knew it, I knew it, even before the race began!

The boys, arms on each other's shoulders, they started jumping and began to spin.

Essie – I'm proud of you, Bonez.

Quigz – Me too, man!

Humbly, Bonez held back a grin.

The scene then broke apart into a few different phases. It started with the announcer giving Bonez some more praises.

Announcer – Bonez is crowned the champ until next year's big race! Congratulations, Bonez, on your exciting win, you truly are an ace!

While the entire crowd was happy and celebrating with some cheers, there was only but one in the entire crowd holding back some tears.

Quigz – Hey Sally, are you alright?

Sally – Quigz, get out of here. I don't want to fight!

After the announcer's announcement, the boys now broke apart. Then a warm hug, coming from behind, touched Bonez's heart.

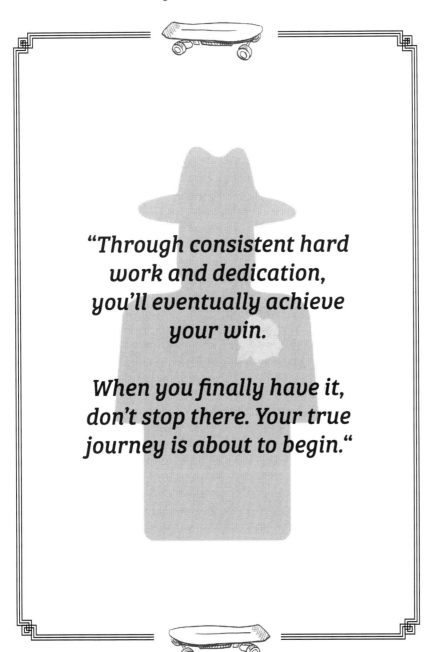

*"Through consistent hard work and dedication, you'll eventually achieve your win.*

*When you finally have it, don't stop there. Your true journey is about to begin."*

# Chapter 7 - In the Parking Lot by Seaview

Peep – Congratulations, Bonez. I'm so happy for you!

Bree – Look here and smile, please, let me get a photo of you two.

Bonez hung out with the two girls, taking photos down in the parking lot. There were different groups of people hanging out, each were in their own spot. Bree took photos of Bonez, of him and his unique shirt with the skeleton boy. Then Bree shot photos of everyone around. It was something she seemed to enjoy.

Quigz went off after Sally, but the Goonsquad got right in his way.

Quigz – I just want to talk to her and see how she's doing.

Goon 1 – Quigz, today's not the day!

At the bottom of the stairs sat a cute group of girls. In front, on his skateboard, Essie was doing some swirls. This was the same group of girls that Essie had seen the other day on the hill. 'Ladies check this out,' he said while showing off his skill.

A flash at that moment caught Essie by the eye. Bree snapped a photo, laughing.

Bree – Hey, check out this guy!

Essie looked over at Bree and was taken back by her style. Tough, confident, and beautiful, she even had a perfect smile.

Bree was Peeps' best friend; they considered themselves cousins from the start. Their parents were friends from high school. Since birth, Peep and Bree were never apart.

Bree was an olive-skinned brunette; she had some freckles scattered on her face. She liked to dress with class and style and always did so with grace.

Essie – Hey, what's up. I'm Essie. I guess you liked those moves that you just saw?

Bree – Poor boy doesn't know when he's being a clown.

Bree said, while laughing, then finished with an 'Awe'.

Confused, Essie and Bonez stood there. Peep, embarrassed, stood as she held back a smile. Bree started talking about Bonez and how she can help him; that went on for a little while.

Bree – A lot of my photos get into the biggest magazines around. I try to cover skateboarding in every town. I shoot photos at every skate event that I happen to attend. Your moves are great, and I love this shirt, to these magazines your photos I'll send.

Essie – Oh, so you're in magazines; but I've never seen a photo shot by someone named Bree.

Bree – You, reading magazines? Don't make me laugh, that's not something I could see.

Essie – Eh, you'd be shocked. I actually read quite a bit. And I've never seen a photo shot by Bree, sorry, that I must admit.

Bree – Yeah, well, have you ever heard of a photographer that goes by the name Breeze-Shots? I've been in Skate-Topia, Shreds, 50/50 and not to mention OG-Spots.

Essie – What, you're Breeze-Shots?!? Get out of town! You're easily my favorite photographer. You have the best shots around!

Bree – Alright, alright, no need to get so excited.

Essie – It's an honor to meet you, I'm truly delighted.

Taken back by Essie's knowledge, Bree was secretly pretty impressed. But she wasn't the type of girl to let you know what she's thinking; her thoughts and feelings she never confessed.

In an attempt to change the topic that she currently had at hand. 'A group photo of all of you!', Bree then began to demand.

Essie, Bonez and Peep stood together. Bree took a few photos of the crew.

Bonez – Come on Bree, get in here. Let's get a photo with you in it too!

'Wait for me!' yelled Quigz, jumping on their backs as he appeared right out of thin air.

Essie – Hey, Quigz, watch yourself! You better not mess up my hair!

Bree snapped a selfie of the crew, almost everyone had a smile on their face. What a nice way to celebrate the win, for Bonez after his downhill race.

# Bonez by: Mr. Roses

Everyone was now starting to disperse, saying good-bye as they each went off on their own way. Before she left, there was one last thing that Peep wanted to say. 'Bonez, before I go, take this,' she said as she handed Bonez a little note. Her phone number and *call me sometime*, was the message that Peep had wrote.

Bonez now stood alone in the parking lot, in joy, as the sun was about to set.

Bonez – What a day! The win and Peep's number, today I'll never forget.

*"Good times with friends
and family never seems
to get old.*

*With genuine care and
good intentions, a happy
life you're sure to mold."*

# CHAPTER 8 – THE PHONES START RINGING

In the middle of a dream, we start this chapter of the book. Bonez is captain of a ship, chasing a fish he's trying to hook. Bonez, all in blue, has a white beard and captain's hat. The fish he's chasing is an interesting one that always seems to chat.

Bonez – On straight ahead, the sound is getting clearer! I can hear the ringing that the fish is making. I think we're getting nearer.

Bonez and his ship's crew have been chasing this fish for what felt like days. The sun was getting strong; you could feel its hot rays. The ringing that the fish was making was now coming from right below.

Bonez – Cast the hook! We're going to get this fish—go, go, go!

The crew on the ship then cast the hook. To hook the fish, not much time it took. For quite a while, they battled to pull the fish up onto the ship. As they pulled the fish up, the boat now started to tip.

Bonez – Come on, crew. We're almost there!

With tons of excitement, Bonez jumped in the air.

Right as the fish was about to break the surface of the water, Bonez woke up to his mom yelling, 'Wow, what an offer!'

Momma Bonez – Gus, get up. How are you even still in bed? The phones been ringing all morning; you won't believe what's being said!

Bonez - Hey. Morning, Mom.

Bonez said while wiping the crust out of his eye.

Momma Bonez – Get yourself dressed and ready. Today these agents are coming by.

Bonez - Who's coming by, and who's been calling on the phone?

Momma Bonez – It's these skateboard companies, they won't leave us alone. Your father's on his way home, and these agents are coming over around two. They have some offers to talk about and seem excited to meet you.

Momma Bonez was a typical mother— caring, loving, and sweet as could be. She'll always help whoever she can, that's something you can guarantee. She was tall, thin, and glowing, a bit nervous but always keeps it together. Her voice was soft and gentle; her words were light as a feather.

Poppa Bonez – Hey, everyone I'm home. Where are you all?

Momma Bonez - We're up in Gus's room honey!

Momma Bonez yelled down the hall.

Poppa Bonez was a gentleman, always wearing a fedora and carrying a briefcase around. Not a thing could get past him, his intelligence was very profound.

He was a serious-faced man, but had a heart that was made of gold.

Poppa Bonez – Listen, guys, when these agents talk, your emotions need to be controlled.

He explained what an agent does and how the process of bargaining goes.

Poppa Bonez – They want to sponsor you, Gus, and for the cheapest deal they'll want to close.

Bonez - They want to sponsor me and add me to their team?!?

Bonez said with much excitement; he even let out a light scream.

Poppa Bonez – Gus, this is what I'm talking about. Around the agents, you must keep your cool. Our calm composure is the key to bargaining; it's a very powerful tool.

Momma Bonez – Gus, I'm so happy for you! This is a very exciting day.

Bonez - I can't wait for the agents to come by and hear what they have to say!

The whole family was excited. They started getting ready for their important guests. They each began to prepare themselves, to be ready for any requests.

Bonez cleaned his room, then he started to get all his skate stuff into order. He was ready to prove to these agents, that he was a great skateboarder. Momma Bonez was in the kitchen, she prepped snacks and anything the agents might want to drink. Poppa Bonez was in his office, quietly trying to think.

In the Bonez household, energy was flowing, and positivity was moving all around. Then they all headed to the front door, as the doorbell began to sound.

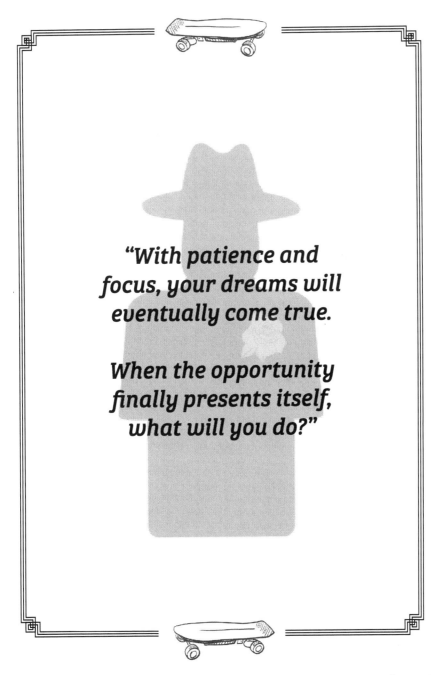

"With patience and
focus, your dreams will
eventually come true.

When the opportunity
finally presents itself,
what will you do?"

# CHAPTER 9 - CATCHING THE FISH

The front door swung open, and there three men stood, all with eager eyes.

Poppa Bonez – Well, hello there, how are you all? Come on in, guys.

One by one, each agent walked in. The first one was tall with a beard and awfully quite thin. The second one was short and chubby with greasy slicked hair. The third one was young and clean-cut, but to the others experience, he probably couldn't compare.

Tall Agent – Well hello there, Bonez, you know you're quite the star. I can see you, in your future, going very far!

Short Agent – Yes, I can see it too; you just need the proper guidance. The way this business works is really just a science.

Bonez stood there, still, and let out a light smirk.

Poppa Bonez – Alright guys, let's take it to the kitchen and get down to some work.

As Momma Bonez started towards the kitchen, the tall and short agents cut her off to lead the way. The young agent stepped back to let Momma Bonez pass; good manners he seemed to display.

Poppa Bonez then stopped Bonez, just as the others were walking away.

 Poppa Bonez – You see that Gus? Actions show true colors. It's not always about what they say.

Inside of the kitchen, all the men sat around a rectangular-shaped table.

Tall Agent – What a magnificent table you have here.

Short Agent – Yes, it's surely quite stable!

Bonez and Poppa Bonez sat next to each other, with their backs towards the cabinets and sink. Momma Bonez was behind them asking 'Would anyone like something to drink'?

The short and tall agents sat on the other side of the table, with their backs against the wall. The young agent sat at the head of the table, he was positioned right next to the hall.

The tall agent went off talking, he spoke very quick.

Tall Agent – I'll get Bonez's face everywhere! That will surely do the trick! I can just see it now, you'll be among all the stars. You'll be doing what you want and driving in fancy cars.

Short Agent – Don't listen to him Bonez. He's not the one who can do it! I'll bring you to stardom—this is how you have to view it. All the fans who will support you, they're really just simpleminded. They'll soon know you're the best skater around, and I'll make sure that they're reminded.

Poppa Bonez – Hmm, both sound interesting gentlemen, but we might have to think about it for a few.

Poppa Bonez looked over at the young agent, 'And now what would you do'?

Chapter 9 - Catching the Fish

The young agent sat up quickly, cleared his throat, and looked a little nervous.

Young Agent - Well, we would sponsor Bonez, and always be of service. I work for 50/50, we're a new skate company that's making its name around. Two years ago, we started the company and kicked it off the ground.

Short Agent – 50/50 skate company! You must be joking, boy!

Laughing along, the tall agent said, 'Bonez's career you'll surely destroy.'

Short Agent – I'm with OG-Spots!

Tall Agent – And I'm with Shreds! You have to hear our theme song—the kids can't get it out of their heads.

Poppa Bonez – Now come on gentlemen, let the boy speak.

Young Agent – We really like your skeleton shirt; it's something that's very unique.

Bonez – Hey, thanks man. It's my favorite shirt. I wear it every day.

Young Agent – We're thinking of making it your logo. So, what do you say?

Poppa Bonez – Well, I'll say this before Gus expresses his mind. First off, young agent, you truly are very kind. Now as it goes for you two, it probably won't work out.

'What!?! What do you mean!?!' said the tall and short agents, as they both began to shout.

Poppa Bonez – Well, of course we've done our research, and your companies have both achieved great success. But that's not what's most important, at least to us, nevertheless. For me you were both out the second you cut my wife off as she began to walk. Not to mention all your grand promises and the larger-than-life talk.

The tall and short agents just sat there; confusion was written all over their face.

Poppa Bonez – Now Gus, what do you think of the young agent's offer? Speak up, now is your place.

Bonez – You seem like a good guy, and I like the ideas about the skeleton boy.

Young Agent – I'll create your clothing, social media, and ads. It's something I'll greatly enjoy.

Poppa Bonez – Well, it sounds like a plan if you had to ask me. Now it's time for you two gentlemen to go, I hope you both agree.

Poppa Bonez exited the kitchen, leading the tall and short agents back to the front door.

Momma Bonez – Bye, gentlemen, thanks for coming!

But her good-bye was something both agents would ignore.

The young agent hung around for a while and showed off his many contacts. He laid out everything he can do for Bonez and went over some of the contracts.

After the papers were signed, with a wave, the young agent went off on his way. With all the thoughts of his dream coming true, the excitement in Bonez's eyes shined bright as a ray.

"*Success and excitement always go hand in hand.*

*Never let money control you, no matter what it can command.*

*Because money comes and money goes, believe me it's true.*

*What's important is genuine relations. With them there's nothing you can't do.*"

# Chapter 9 - Catching the Fish

# Chapter 10 - The Phone Call

Ring, ring, ring, then finally she picked up the phone.

Peep - Hello, who's there?

Peep answered swiftly, all in a very sweet tone.

Bonez – Hey, Peep, it's Bonez. How was your day?

Peep – Hey, Bonez! Thanks for asking, today was okay. And how was your day? Did you get contacted by anyone?

Bonez - Yeah and signed a contract; the deal's already done.

Peep - Wow, Bree said they'd call you immediately, but I didn't think she meant so fast.

Bonez - It's a day I've been dreaming of for a while now, and I can't believe it's come at last.

Bonez went on for a few, explaining all the things that his new agent said.

Bonez – All the stuff he talked about, I can't get it out of my head.

Peep – That all sounds pretty cool, especially about the sponsorship and all of the gear. Your own backpack, shirts and shoes—I'll definitely make sure to wear. Bree also said you would be on social media, that they would advertise your stuff all over the internet.

Bonez – Hopefully. The agent said working with 50/50 is something I'll never regret.

Bonez – So, now getting back to you, how did you set up your room? I'm sure it's filled with bright colors and smells of tons of perfume.

Peep – Ha, I guess you could say that. You pretty much nailed it on the head. Each of my walls is a different color: green, blue, yellow and red. I have a bed, couch, dresser, two closets, oh and I have a few of Bree's photos on my wall. Most are big scenic photos she took, and I have a few photos of me and her that are small.

Bonez – Nice, sounds like a comfortable room with many pleasant reminders.

Peep – Oh, and I have some awesome butterflies, that I painted on my window blinders.

Listening to Peep talk put a smile on Bonez's face.

Peep – And what about you? How did you set up your space?

Bonez – My room has a blue ceiling and the walls are painted gray. I have a rack that holds my skateboards, horizontally is how they lay. I have a tv, video games, and a bean bag, that's where I sit when I'm not skating around.

I have skate posters and a solid radio that puts off a pretty good sound.

Peep listened to Bonez and was comforted by his voice. She could listen to him for forever, if she only had the choice.

Bonez – Besides all that, there's a reason I called more than just to simply say hi. Essie, Quigz, and myself are heading to the skate park tomorrow. You and Bree should both come by.

Peep – Sounds like a plan, I'm excited for the day!

Bonez felt at peace; there wasn't much more he had to say.

Bonez – Great! So, I'll see you tomorrow, Peep. Hope you have a nice night.

Peep – Same to you Bonez. Thanks for the call, and again thanks for tomorrow's invite!

"In this world there's always that person, who for you they are the one.

That when you meet them and get to know them, the connections can't be undone.

And if you find them, your surely lucky because not every one does.

Finding that person is everything, you'll even forget how life without them was."

# Chapter 10 - The Phone Call

Bonez by: Mr. Roses

# Chapter 11 - The Skate Park

Over a smooth bump, Bonez picked up a bit of speed. Riding on his banana board with some style is how he continued to proceed.

He went of a ramp and lifted into the air. He spun around quickly, all without a care.

Bonez - Wow, did you see that one?

Quigz - I can't believe my eyes!

Essie - Another new trick. Of course, we saw it! Nothing

62

you do catches me by surprise.

Bonez was skating Letitbe's skate park; it was located at the center of town. It had ramps and bumps and curved walls. It was a fun spot to cruise all around.

Essie waved down Bonez. When he came over, Essie began to speak.

Essie – Look, it's the girls. And check out Bree's skateboard—that design is pretty unique.

Peep and Bree entered into the park. Bree's skateboard was painted to look like a shark.

Bree stood on her skateboard, standing stiff as could be. Frustration on her face was all that you could see.

Bree held on to Peep's arm as she rolled on the pavement.

Bonez and Essie walk towards the girls, and Essie began his statement.

Essie – Hey ladies, how are you doing today? And Bree, look at you, that's some stance I must say.

Bree – Mind your own business. I'll figure out what I need to do!

Bonez – Hey, how are you doing Peep? It's nice to see you.

Peep – Hey Bonez, how are you guys doing? Today's one of summers perfect days. Not a cloud in the sky, and the sun's shining brightly. I love the feeling of its warm rays.

Essie – Sorry, didn't mean to get you mad, Bree. Here let me show you a little trick.

As Essie went to grab Bree's hand, she slapped his hand away quick.

Bree, appearing serious, Essie and Bonez looking confused as ever. Always smiling, Peep gets a kick out of Bree; she's been dealing with her attitude since forever.

To break the awkward moment, Peep jumped in and began to say.

Peep – Hey guys, where's Quigz? He's not hanging out with us today?

Now we flash on over inside of a bush. Crawling on his stomach, through it, Quigz began to push. The bush was located on the other side of the park. Hidden in the shade, the lighting was dark.

On the other side of the bush was a bench. There was Sally and the tough Goonsquad. Quigz thought to himself 'I don't know what it is, but something about Sally seems very odd.'

Usually Sally would be skating the park, yelling and pushing everyone out of her way. Now she sat alone on the bench, without a single word to say.

Quigz – Hmm, maybe she's still upset about the race. Let's see if a scare can lead her to a chase.

Quigz jumped out of the bush and scared the life out of

the four. But the reaction experienced was something he never thought was in store.

Instead of getting mad and chasing Quigz, Sally screamed and ran in the other direction. The Goonsquad then got right in Quigz's face; they were there for Sally's protection.

Goon 1 – One of these days, Quigz, you're going to get it, man! You think your jokes are always so great? Sally's in a weird spot now, man. If you keep this up, you'll become someone she really does hate.

Quigz stood there and took in all the words that were being said. All while the Goonsquad held him, giving him a noogie on his head. Quigz was the youngest of many brothers, so this treatment was nothing new.

Quigz – Ugh, I feel so bad for Sally, there must be something that I could do.

Peep – Oh, no! Look over there, the Goonsquad's rub-

bing their knuckles on Quigz's head!

Bonez – Look at his face; he's calm as a pickle. It must have been something he said.

Also at this moment, a rare occurrence was taking place. Essie was helping Bree skate, and his lessons she seemed to embrace.

Peep – Wow, this is strange. Bree being nice to a boy isn't in her style. She usually puts up a wall; it must have been Essie's smile.

Bonez – Hmm, well anyways while we have a moment, I wanted to ask you out on a date. I was thinking down by the ice cream shop, maybe tonight around eight?

With butterflies in her stomach, Peep said, 'Sounds perfect, I'm in'. Bonez said, 'Great' while smiling and also feeling butterflies within.

*"When your days are happy and you seem to be getting lucky. Good news you're on the right rout.*

*Just stay humble and keep on working, soon you'll find what life's all about."*

# Chapter 11 - The Skate Park

Bonez by: Mr. Roses

# Chapter 12 – Date Night

The town of Letitbe is an interesting one, oh yes that's for sure. It was made of cliffs, hills, and beaches; let me give you a little tour.

Houses were scattered around the hill, and all of the streets led down to the shoreline. At the top it is connected to another town, built down a cliff is Letitbe's design.

In the middle was the skate park, and right next to it was the school. At recess you can go to the skate park; all the kids thought that was pretty cool.

Chapter 12 - Date Night

At the bottom of the hill was the beach that we all know as Seaview. The East side was Kent Street with its cliffs that the skaters had to race through.

Andrews Street was less steep on the West, it had a few stores that were scattered around. At the end by the water was the ice cream shop; out front was where Peep and Bonez were found.

The ice cream shop was a unique building, mint blue with a huge cone on the top. On the side, by the water, was a window; during the summer, that's where everyone goes to shop.

Bonez was in his usual skeleton boy shirt. Peep was wearing purple polka-dot pants and a baggy white shirt that matched her shoes.

Bonez – Do you want sprinkles on your ice cream cone, Peep?

Peep – It doesn't matter to me, Bonez; you can choose.

Now walking towards the beach, Bonez and Peep had both finished eating their sprinkle-covered ice cream cone.

Peep – So, where did your parents get your name from? You're the only Bonez I've ever known.

Bonez – Well, actually my name's Gus—that's something not many people know. The nickname started with my first skeleton boy shirt, but that was a long time ago.

Peep – Gus, I like that. The name definitely suits you.

Bonez – Well, if you want, you can call me it, but you'll be among the few.

Peep and Bonez were now sitting on the beach. Peep was running her fingers through the sand. Cool, breezy, and a full moon, this night couldn't have been better planned.

Bonez – So, tell me a little bit about you, Peep. What are the things that you like to do? What are your days like, is there any hobbies you've found that are new?

Peep – Usually, I just hang out in my room, listening to music, and actually, I just started to paint a bit. It seems like I'll be painting more now, especially since Bree's about to split.

Bonez – Where is she going, what do you mean?

Peep – Her and her family are off; they have to follow the skate scene. Since the start of summer when Bree got big with the photos, things haven't been the same. Now they travel all over in an RV, for your skate competition is the only reason they came.

Sitting, holding her legs, staring blankly, Peep rested her chin on her knees. Sadness was building in Peep's eyes. Quietly sitting next to her, this is what Bonez now sees.

Peep – I used to hang out with Bree every day. But this is good for her and her family, so what else is there to say.

Bonez – Well, what about other friends, is there anyone else you hang out with besides Bree?

Peep – Not really, because of my style, the other girls are always judging me.

Bonez – Well, what about your parents, at least they're there for you.

Peep – Not really, they're usually working. They always have something important to do.

Feeling bad for Peep, Bonez tried to think of something to say.

Bonez – Don't worry Peep, all these feelings will soon go away. My parents always say life's like the phases of the moon. Your days will have ups and downs, it's important to get yourself in-tune.

Peep – I don't understand, can you explain what you mean?

Bonez – Life's full of ups and downs, there's barely any in-between. Sometimes the moon's bright and full, those are your best days. Sometimes the moon's dark and lonely, that's when life feels like you're in a haze. So, we have to appreciate the good days, because soon they will be gone. Plus, the bad days won't last forever either, they'll get better at the break of dawn.

Looking over at Bonez, Peep felt comforted by what he said. Bonez put his arm around Peep; on his shoulder, she rested her head.

Bonez and Peep had a moment where they both felt whole. Life slowed down for a minute; it felt like everything was in their control.

Then something shocking caught Peep's eye. Essie and Bree were by the water, casually just walking by.

Peep – Hey, you two, you're just not going to say hello?

Different reactions from Essie and Bree, they both began to show.

Essie was happy and waving. Bree, embarrassed, hid her smile. They walked over to Bonez and Peep and hung out for quite a while.

*"Some days are happy and bright, some days are lonely and gray.*

*Keep yourself focused on the positive thoughts and take it day by day."*

76

# Chapter 12 - Date Night

# Chapter 13 - The End of Summer

The last few days of summer, the crew pretty much hung out every day. From days at the skate park into evenings by the ice cream shop, they watched the sunset's beautiful display.

Bonez mostly hung out with Peep. Essie mostly hung out with Bree. Quigz rode the fifth wheel, and Sally was no-where to be.

Quigz – Guys, this is weird—she's nowhere in sight! It's the last day of summer. She should be here, right?

The crew was at the skate park, Quigz was dressed in yellow to imitate Sally's style.

Bonez – Maybe she's still bummed from the race, the re-match isn't for quite a while.

Essie – I read this one article about what failure could do to a person. It could crush your confidence and make the chances of trying again worsen.

Bree – Yeah, well I read an article about how it should motivate the heck out of you. Failures are just lessons leading you to what you truly have to do.

Quigz – I feel bad for Sally. I need to break her out of her funk.

Bree – I don't understand why you care about her, Quigz. Sally's nothing but just a punk.

Quigz – Ha, I know what you mean but Sally actually has a good heart. Because of where she comes from, being tough is pretty smart.

Bree – Where she comes from, what do you mean?

Quigz – She lives in an orphanage; it's not the best scene.

Peep – Don't worry, Quigz, next time you see Sally I'm sure you'll put a smile on her face! Just do something nice for her. Maybe get some flowers that she could put in a vase?

The rest of the day was another great one, just like the past few. Skateboarding and hanging out together was all that the crew had to do.

Bonez and Essie rode the skate park. Quigz picked yellow flowers that he planned to give to Sally tomorrow at school. Peep and Bree shot some photos of each other. Then something happened that was pretty cool.

A kid from the skate park, who had spikey hair that looked pretty unique. Walked on over, right up to Bonez, and then began to speak.

Skate Park Kid – Hey excuse me, are you Bonez from 50/50? Your photos on their page are really pretty nifty. I just checked out your social media and added you as a friend. The skeleton boy on your shirt is sweet; I could see it being a new trend.

Caught off guard, a feeling of excitement began to rise. Then the next few things that happened really caught Bonez by surprise.

Bonez – Yeah, that's me. I'm Bonez, in the flesh.

Skate Park Kid - I knew it, I knew it! Your moves are really fresh!

Looking back to his friends, the Skate Park Kid yelled, 'Guys I told you it's him!' Then the first feeling of fame for Bonez now started to begin.

From the enthusiasm of the Skate Park Kid, pretty much everyone headed over to Bonez. Each with tons of excitement on their faces, some were even taking photos on their phones.

Essie, Peep, Bree, and pretty much the entire skate park were by Bonez and created a circle around him. A nervous type of excitement was building, which Bonez could feel within.

Peep watched, shocked at all the action. Bree smirked, satisfied with what she sees. Essie stood next to Bonez smiling, and Quigz was off distracted climbing some trees.

Quigz - Holy cow, I can't believe my eyes! Look at that thing, I can't believe its size!

From the tree, Quigz could see outside of the skate park, as he looked just down the road. Bonez's face, the skeleton boy, and his social media, was what the billboard showed.

'Wow, how awesome is that?' said Peep, as she and Bree stood, excited, next to the boys.

Bree – Don't forget who shot the photo of you, Bonez. That billboard should make a good amount of noise.

Buzzing in excitement, Bonez felt like he was standing alone. Even though everyone in the park was around him, he was lost, deep in his own zone.

Checking his social media, Bonez's friend requests were out the door. He even had some messages from the young agent, one was saying that his merchandise was now in store. Another message said to be ready for tomorrow; that it should be quite the event. Outside of the school, bright and early, 50/50 would be there to represent.

Bonez stood there, silent, with a smile forming on his face. The excitement of his dreams coming true, he would finally start to embrace.

The rest of the day at the skate park, Bonez felt like he was the man. Everything he'd ever dreamed of was now going according to plan.

Tomorrow was the first day of school. Bonez and Peep planned to walk together in the morning. Fame was just around the corner, and a change in Bonez was forming.

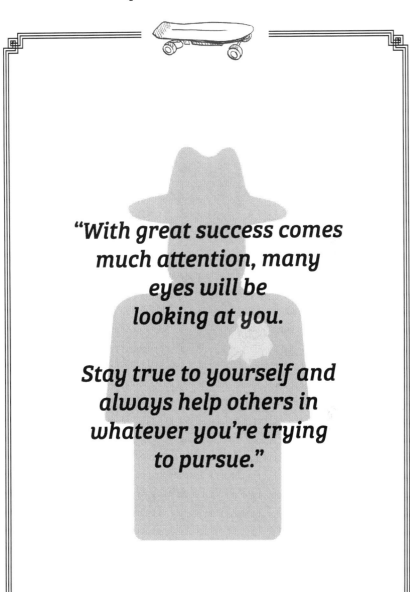

*"With great success comes much attention, many eyes will be looking at you.*

*Stay true to yourself and always help others in whatever you're trying to pursue."*

# Chapter 14 – The First Day of School

The crisp smell of bacon got Bonez right out of bed. The thoughts of what school will be like, he couldn't get out of his head.

Washed up and dressed quickly, Bonez headed out of his room to get some food. Dancing and humming as he entered the kitchen.

Momma Bonez – It sure seems like someone's in a good mood.

Bonez – Morning, Mom. I guess you could say that. Morning, Dad.

At the table, next to Poppa Bonez, is where Bonez sat.

Poppa Bonez – Morning, Gus. Are you excited for the day? I saw an article in the paper about you. 50/50 will be at your school with a little display.

Bonez – Of course, I'm excited. It seems like I'm becoming quite the star. I'm getting friend requests from people I don't know. I must say, it's pretty bizarre.

## Chapter 14 - The First Day of School

Poppa Bonez – Well, that's great news, Gus. Just remember they're not all really your friends. Although most of them will act like it until the excitement finally ends.

Momma Bonez – Listen to your father, Gus. He knows a thing or two. Just follow your heart when making decisions in whatever you're trying to pursue.

After a quick breakfast, Bonez headed out of the house and skated down the street. Just down the road, in front of her gray house, was where he and Peep planned to meet.

Peep - Morning, Gus.

Peep said with a smile.

Bonez – Morning, Peep. I like today's style.

Pink shirt, white pants, yellow shoes. 'Check this out,' Peep said as she began to spin. She painted a skeleton boy on the back of her shirt.

Peep – What do you think? Now I'm your twin!

'Not bad!' Bonez said with a smile, as he and Peep started to walk down the road. Whenever the two hung out together, it always seemed like time had slowed.

Bonez by: Mr. Roses

Letitbe's streets were beautiful. They were hilly and filled with many trees. There are colorful flowers, many bushes and birds, not to mention always a nice breeze.

Bonez only lived a few blocks from Peep, and Peep only lived a few blocks from the school. They walked past Bonez's billboard.

Peep – I have to say, this really is so cool.

Bonez – Yeah, but still a little weird. It's hard to believe it's me.

Peep – Yeah, but what a great photo of you Gus, and I'm sure anyone would agree!

Approaching the school, Bonez and Peep rounded the last block. With the sound of music growing, the next sight had them both in shock.

Outside of the school, by the skate park, 50/50 had set up a stand. All dressed in black-and-white skeleton outfits, 50/50 even had a small band.

Playing "welcome back to school" music, while 50/50's young agent gave out skeleton boy stickers to everyone around. As Bonez and Peep walked over to the stand, "the champ is here" song began to sound.

Bonez and Peep walked into the grand entrance that 50/50 had prepared. Bonez was filled with much excitement, while Peep held on to his arm feeling scared.

Music was playing, people were cheering, and everything almost felt like a blur. This was the start of many things that took Bonez's mind off of her.

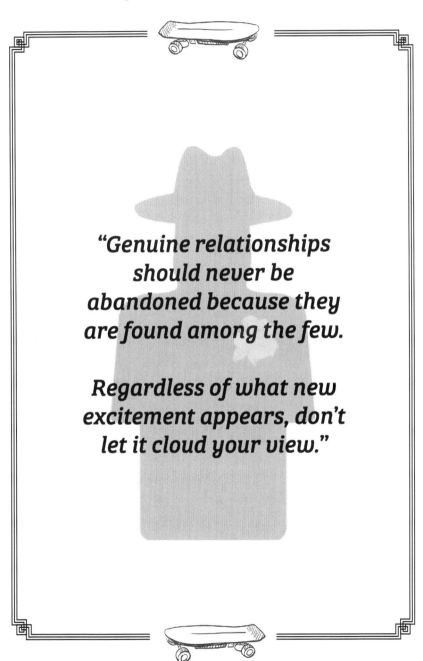

*"Genuine relationships should never be abandoned because they are found among the few.*

*Regardless of what new excitement appears, don't let it cloud your view."*

# Chapter 15 – First Few Weeks of School

Letitbe's school was massive; it had many students and held many different grades. From preschool to college were the classes it held; you were there for nearly two decades.

At the center of the town, next to the skate park, tall, Letitbe's school stood. It was made of bricks, stone, glass—oh and had big arches that were made of wood.

Long and crowded were the hallways, and there were many, many rooms. There's always much excitement inside the building, especially when the new school year resumes.

The first few weeks of school, things weren't the same. Bonez was getting lost and caught up, all in his brand-new fame.

All of the kids in school started wearing his shirts, backpacks, and any new gear. As Bonez walked through the halls, or wherever he was, his name was all you would hear.

Much attention and many compliments were constantly given to Bonez. And everyone had a skeleton boy sticker; most had it on the back of their phones.

Bonez by: Mr. Roses

Walking down the halls together, Bonez, Essie, and Quigz would head to their class. Always surrounded by tons of kids, right past Peep they would pass.

The past few times that Peep talked with Bonez, time no longer slowed. Alone to class, Peep walked the halls, since Bree was back out on the road.

A tough time for Peep, that it was, for sure. Bree was gone again, out taking photos on the skate tour. Usually by herself, Peep now spent most of her days. Painting and drawing to occupy her time, Peep was living, drifting in a haze.

Quigz was still Quigz, in his own world, but something still wasn't right. Since he scared her, by jumping out of the bush, Sally hasn't been anywhere in sight. Not one day at school, has Sally appeared to show her face. Yet every day, Quigz still brings flowers, for Sally to put in a vase.

At times, Essie would get caught up in all the excitement, while hanging out with Bonez and his new fame. Now even some of the older girls that he didn't know started to know his name. But that didn't matter too much to Essie, because he and Bree still talked every day. Constantly texting back and forth, true affection they seemed to display.

Bree was out on the road with her parents; she was following the skate scene. Homeschool, taking photos, and texting Essie, that was her daily routine. Usually she would be texting Peep too, but since meeting Essie that had slowed down quite a bit. Bree and Peep's friendship was distancing, this is something both girls would admit.

Bonez's personality was changing, with many comments from others filling his head. 'You're the best, you're the cutest,' are some of the things that they said.

After school, Bonez was always skating, either the streets, the skate park, or 50/50's main shop. Constantly taking photos and making videos for 50/50, the skate life never seemed to stop.

Bonez by: Mr. Roses

Every few days that passed, on social media 50/50 would put out a new post. The young agent even got Bonez on a TV interview, with a live audience and a host.

Bonez was surely becoming quite famous—him and his shirt with that little skeleton boy. People from all over started to know him, and that was something he seemed to enjoy.

*"Excitement, excitement it will capture some of the best.*

*It will come with success and the excitement of others being expressed.*

*Just know that life's a game and that there is always a test.*

*Stay true to yourself and remember what's important, that I humbly suggest."*

# Chapter 16 - The Lunchroom

On line in the cafeteria, we catch Quigz. He is balancing Jell-O on his head. In his right hand, he balanced a tray that had an apple, macaroni, and two pieces of bread. Even on one foot he stood, then slowly started crouching low. But he didn't have enough strength to stand back up, tipping, he started to yell, 'Oh no!'

As you could imagine, Quigz made quite a mess. Out of the kitchen, jumped a lunch lady: 'Quigz! How could I have guessed'!?!

Lunch Lady – What are we going to do with you, Quigz? This is the second time this week. And let me guess, the balancing act, on your opposite foot that is weak.

Quigz – I almost got it! Just lost my balance as I was trying to stand up.

Lunch Lady – Well maybe practice with an empty tray, and instead of Jell-O, maybe an empty cup?

Shaking his head, Essie looks at Bonez and said, 'Wow what a waste.'

Essie - When I finally open my own restaurant, only on the table is where Quigz's food will be placed.

Bonez and Essie are standing across the lunchroom, holding their trays, while watching Quigz's interesting scene.

Essie – Eh, but I have to say, in Quigz's defense, he's definitely making sure the floor gets clean.

Laughing at Essie's comments, Bonez shook his head and said, 'Yeah, I guess I agree.'

Bonez – So I have to ask, how have things been going? Are you still talking with Bree?

Essie – Yeah, going great. Honestly, I think she might be the one. When I talk with her, everything seems natural. I think the dating scene and I might be done. I support her with her photography, she supports my cooking hobby and dream of opening a restaurant of my own. She really is the best girl, besides my mom, that I think I've ever known.

Bonez – Nice, man, I'm glad to hear. That's what my parents say it's all about. That's how it was for me and Peep, but this fame is something different without a doubt. Girls from all over have been adding me on social media; they all want to be my friend. And the amount of comments and messages I get daily, they never seem to end.

Essie – That definitely is something crazy. So, how does it affect things with you and Peep? Over the summer, you guys seemed to be forming something that looked pretty deep.

Bonez – Yeah, I try to talk with her here and there, but we don't really hang out too much anymore. Since I became famous and am constantly skating, things have been different between us for sure.

Essie – Well, she's right over there, sitting alone, if you want to go say hello.

Bonez – Yeah, I'll go say hi, but I'm still sitting with you and everyone else though.

Essie walked over to the popular kids' table and sat down with his tray and his food. Quigz was on the floor, cleaning the mess he made. Always laughing, he even got the lunch lady in a good mood.

Bonez started walking over to Peep, she had her back to him and was dressed in all gray. Standing next to the table, he didn't sit, as he quickly thought of something to say.

Bonez by: Mr. Roses

Bonez – Hey, Peep, long time no talk. How are things?

Peep – Hey, not bad, Gus. How are you, and everything that fame brings?

Bonez – Yeah, everything's been pretty crazy, that I can't lie. Sorry I haven't stopped by in a while, not even just to say hi.

Peep – It's ok. I know you're busy and have many other things that are going on.

Then a loud yell from the popular table,

Popular Girl – Hey, Bonez, come on!

Ignoring the popular girl's comment, Bonez continued, 'So what have you been up to?'

Peep – Just painting and drawing and listening to music. What else is there to do?

Bonez could sense in Peep's demeanor that something wasn't right. Just looking at this all-gray outfit, she would never wear something not bright. Bonez felt in his stomach that he should stay awhile and see what was wrong with Peep.

Peep – Oh, Gus, before I forget—I made something for you to keep.

Reaching in her backpack, Peep looked for the drawing she made yesterday at home. Now, after a second yell from the popular girl, Bonez's mind started to roam.

Bonez – Ugh, hey Peep, so how about you show me that drawing later at recess?

Shortness and lack of attention, Bonez began to express.

Heading towards the popular kids' table, Bonez touched Peep's shoulder as he started to walk away. A feeling of emptiness as she sat alone, Peep didn't have anything to say.

*"When we go through life while following our instincts, things tend to always work out.*

*The second we resist and ignore our instincts, troubles coming, that's without a doubt."*

# Chapter 16 - The Lunchroom

# CHAPTER 17 - RECESS

After lunch, inside of the skate park, everyone was scattered around. Bonez and Essie sat on the bench with the popular kids. By the flowers is where Quigz was found.

Peep sat by herself on some grass; she was leaning on the fence that surrounded the park. In his own world, picking flowers for Sally, Quigz overheard a loud remark.

Goon 1 - Let's go boys, let's shred away! All of you kids skating the park, you better get out of our way!

Looking over quick, Quigz was shocked to see the Goonsquad inside the park skating.

Quigz - Finally! I hope they know where Sally is. I can't just keep on waiting.

The Goonsquad was a tough group that unfortunately didn't like to go to school. Though when Sally was around, she made sure they went; going to school was her number one rule. The Goonsquad brothers lived at the orphanage with Sally and were each one year apart. None of the other orphans cared to go to school; Sally was the only one who was smart.

Quigz hasn't seen the Goonsquad in a while either, at least not since the day he scared them by jumping out of the bush. Quigz walked over to grab their attention, but they skated past and knocked him down with a push.

Quigz – Hey, what was that for!?! I just have a question to ask you!

Goon 1 – Yeah, well, if we don't wanna answer, what are you gonna do?!?

Quigz, looking sad and serious, said, 'I just want to know if Sally's alright.'

Quigz - I haven't seen her in a while. I'm not here looking for a fight.

Goon 1 – Alright, Quigz, take it easy. You look like you're a second away from some waterworks. I don't know what it is that Sally sees in you; you really have some weird quirks. Sally's back at the orphanage, and if she's not going to school, neither are we. Now get out of our way and let us skate, or you'll catch a beating from us three!

Feeling a little relieved, Quigz planned to go see Sally at the orphanage on top of the hill. His mind was racing in every direction as he stood very still. He thought about what he would say to Sally, and how she might react. Quigz was determined to break Sally out of her funk, this surely was a fact.

Deep in her own thoughts, we now look over to Peep. She was looking at the drawing she made that she wanted Bonez to keep. It was a drawing from the first date that they both went on together. She thought about how she felt that night, and how when she hung out with Bonez, she felt better.

Peep – Gus said sometimes the moon is dark and lonely; that's when life feels like you're living in a haze. But not to worry because it won't last forever; soon there will be better days.

Since the fame, Bonez hasn't been himself, but Peep knew that he had a good heart somewhere inside. She couldn't just let their relationship fall apart, she needed to know that at least she tried.

With a feeling of hope, Peep quickly jumped up to her feet. She walked over to Bonez, Essie, and the popular kids, but didn't get a pleasant greet.

Popular Girl – Ugh, who brought you over here? And what's with the clothes, why all gray?

Used to the criticism from the popular girls, Peep didn't have anything to say.

'Alright, please, calm down girls,' Bonez seemed to command.

Bonez – Hey, Peep, I was just looking for you. Is that the drawing you have in your hand?

Nodding her head and smiling, Peep said, 'Yes it's the drawing I did for you.' She happily handed over the picture and waited to see what Bonez would do.

Bonez looked down at the drawing. Essie and the popular kids leaned in to see Peep's art. Then a warm feeling grew large inside and began to touch Bonez's heart.

It was a drawing of the view they had on the night of their first date. The moon shined brightly off the ocean, as that night started to get late. At the bottom of the drawing was the beach, and sitting on the sand was Bonez and Peep.

Peep – I hope you like it, Gus. I made it for you to keep.

Right at that moment, a question came about.

'"Gus"!?! Who is that?!?' the popular girl began to shout.

As we learned earlier in the story, not many people knew Bonez as Gus. A nervous feeling came over him; he didn't want the popular girl to make a fuss. Scared that he might lose the image he has as the cool skater guy. Speaking quickly, Bonez brushed Peep away; he couldn't even look her in the eye.

Bonez – Nothing, it's just a joke. Don't pay attention to what she has to say. Ugh, and hey, Peep, thanks for the drawing. We'll talk another day.

Peep turned around quickly. Embarrassed, she started to walk away. Again, she felt empty inside, and again she had nothing to say. It was clear that Bonez didn't care about her; all he cared about was his image and the fame. Unfortunately, Peep now knew that things between her and Bonez were no longer the same..

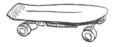

*"When we fall off our path, life always has a way to guide us back and restart.*

*It could be in the form of an idea that excites us and touches us deep in our heart.*

*It could be an opportunity presenting itself that we should take if we're smart.*

*If we resist and go against our instincts, then we're sure to fall apart."*

# Chapter 17 - Recess

# Chapter 18 - The Orphanage

It was right after school, Bonez, Essie and Quigz were walking through some trees. Acorns on the ground, hills leading up, this is what the crew now sees.

They were heading towards Letitbe's orphanage; it was located at the top of the hill. Through the trees is the quickest way up; when skating the streets, this was their normal drill.

Essie – Yeah, man, I don't know what I'm going to do. This beefing with Bree is something tough to go through. In my defense, I didn't do anything wrong. I just liked another girl's video; on the guitar, she was playing my favorite song.

Bonez – Ha, girls, what could you do? Just go meet another one, at least that's my view.

Essie – Eh, maybe. Bree's telling me she wants a break. This terrible feeling inside, I can no longer take. I mean I really do like her, but she wants to focus on her photography and herself. So I may as well do what I want, talk to other girls and focus on myself!

Bonez – That's the spirit! I'll introduce you to some girls at tomorrow's skate event. After skating and hanging with me, you'll meet another girl, one hundred percent.

Quigz was walking ahead of Bonez and Essie. He was listening to everything being said. Right at that moment, if you looked at his face, it was redder than the hair on his head. Even though Quigz was a little crazy, he believed in love and had an old genuine soul. He picked up two acorns and threw them at the boys; his anger he couldn't control.

After being hit in the head with the acorns, Bonez and Essie stopped and looked over at Quigz. They quickly picked up acorns to throw back, and Quigz took off running through the twigs.

Running up the hill, the boys were laughing. They were in the middle of a little acorn war. There was dodging and jumping and hiding behind trees; there was even one point where Quigz dropped down to the floor.

Essie – Go ahead Quigz, keep running up the hill!

The boys were having fun; this seemed to be quite a thrill.

Suddenly Quigz stopped running. Essie and Bonez caught up and stood right next to him. They all stared up at an old building that looked very grim. The orphanage looked blackish gray, but you could tell that wasn't its original color. It had cracks; it had weeds; it had an old swing set; and it even had a hanging gutter.

Quigz – Is that really the orphanage? It almost looks like an abandoned building.

Bonez – Yeah, I hear you Quigz. It even looks like it's tilting.

Right at that moment there was a loud slam. The back door swung open and out Sally ran. She was holding her big yellow skateboard and was being chased by another girl and some young boy.

Sally – Please, you can't have my skateboard! It's not just a toy!

Orphan Girl – You better give it to us Sally. My little brother wants to give it a shot.

Little Brother – Yeah, and you don't want us to do what we did last time, have you already forgot?

Sally had a flashback to the girl pulling her hair and the little brother wiping his boogers on her clothes.

Sally – Please, just don't break it, and I guess I'll let you ride it for a little, I suppose.

The two took Sally's skateboard and both walked away. Sally, feeling defeated and down, she didn't have anything to say. She walked over to the swing set and sat swinging as she kicked the dirt.

Quigz – Guys, I think I should go talk to her by myself. She clearly seems very hurt.

*"You should never judge a book by its cover because you might just learn something that's new.*

*The same goes for people because you never know the things that they've been through."*

# Chapter 18 - The Orphanage

# Chapter 19 - Quigz and Sally

Quigz started to walk over towards Sally. Bonez and Essie headed back down the hill. Quigz walked slowly, as he thought of what to say, but slipped on some leaves and took quite the spill.

Sally looked over at the noise she heard and yelled, "Hey, what are you doing here?!?' Quigz stood up quickly, with a white sock in hand, and waved it in the air.

# Chapter 19 - Quigz and Sally

Quigz – I come in peace. I'm just here to say hi. I was wondering how you were doing, so I thought I'd stop by.

Sally – Listen, Quigz, I don't know what you planned to come up here and say. But I think it would be best if you just walked away.

A little discouraged, Quigz reached into his back pocket and pulled out some yellow flowers.

Quigz – These are for you Sally. Sorry they're a little crushed, they've been in my pocket for a few hours.

Quigz walked over to the swing set and handed Sally the flowers. She took the pretty bunch from Quigz and down fell some tear showers.

Quigz quickly sat in the swing next to Sally and said, 'Hey, are you alright?' She was timid, sensitive, and weak. Quigz has never seen Sally in this light.

Sally – Yeah, I'm alright, just having a moment. I never would have expected something this nice from my biggest opponent.

Quigz – Sally, I'm not your opponent. I like to mess with you because I thought we both saw it as fun. If that's not the case, and you want me to stop, then believe me I'm done.

Bonez by: Mr. Roses

Sally, smiling, said, 'No, it's alright Quigz, I get a kick out of the crazy things that you do.' Quigz smiled back, as he rocked on the swing, and said, 'So, what has happened to you?'

Sally – I don't know. It all just wasn't meant to be. This is where I belong, in this run-down orphanage, don't you see?

Quigz – No, I don't. I don't see it at all. This isn't anyone's dream, at least not anyone I could recall.

Sally – Well, it's not my dream either. You just don't understand the things that I've been through.

Quigz – Yeah, you're right, I don't. But I do wish I knew.

Sally, lost in her emotions, has felt alone and abandoned in the world. As she thought deeply on what to say; her hair she pulled and twirled.

Sally – Well, just look at my life, and you could see it all. I'm never going to escape this place; my chances are very small. Most of these orphans are failures, and I guess I'm one and the same. Like I said, this is my life; I guess I'm not meant for the fame.

Quigz – Sally, I'm not going to lie, I'm really not sure what happened that made you change. Just a little while ago you were your usual self, now you're acting very strange.

Sally – I was Letitbe's top skater until last summer when Bonez came and took my title away. I was on my way to being sponsored like Bonez, and now I'm stuck here to stay.

Not to the fault of the orphans, their mindset was unfortunately very poor. Embedded in their minds was that they were failures, deep down to their core.

Since the day Sally lost the race down Kent Street, the other orphans haven't let her live it down. They would constantly pick on and tease her, while reminding her she's no longer the best in town.

Bonez by: Mr. Roses

The other orphans didn't go to school; they were mean and never thought about what their lives could be. The only ones who were nice to Sally were those Goonsquad brothers of three.

Quigz – So, this is all because of the race? Because you weren't the one who won? Come on, Sally, don't be silly— skateboard races are supposed to be fun!

Sally – Quigz, like I said, you don't understand. Skating was the only thing that didn't make me feel like a failure. Now even that's slipped out of my hand.

Quigz – Yeah, but failure isn't defeat, it's just a chance to start again. Everything happens for a reason; maybe it just wasn't your time then.

Inside of Sally, a slight sense of optimism began to rise. Looking at Sally, Quigz could see it in her eyes.

Quigz – Listen, I've never been an orphan, and I'm sure it could be quite tough. But no matter where you are, life could always be quite rough. I mean, look at me, I have a nice family but I'm the youngest of fifteen brothers and sisters. Every day I get ignored or picked on, and I'm left with bumps and blisters.

Sally – Sounds kind of rough. I guess that's why you like to act tough.

122

Quigz said, 'It's not just an act!' While smiling with a grin. "Just look at these guns,' he said while flexing. 'I've been hitting the gym!'

A blush on Sally's face started to appear. Sally's mood was changing, and to Quigz this was very clear.

Quigz – Sally, how about tomorrow you stop by 50/50's downhill skate event. It's just for fun and to promote skateboarding, that's the only intent. And maybe you should start going back to school, if not for you, at least for those three Goonsquad brothers. Your actions don't only affect you; they also affect others.

Touched by Quigz's words and his genuine concern. Sally made the decision that it was time for her return. She planned to go to 50/50's downhill skate event tomorrow and to return back to school. Now it was time to get her skateboard back; her confidence and strength Quigz helped fuel.

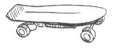

"Not everyone lives the
same life, not everyone
experiences happy days.

But with the right
mindset and a drive, there
is always different ways.

That is to change your
life because we're always
able to decide on what we
want it to be.

Don't let situations or
others hold you down.
Everyone has the right
to be free."

# Chapter 19 - Quigz and Sally

# Chapter 20 - 50/50 Downhill Skate Event

On a crisp sunny morning, 50/50 hosted their downhill skate event. All skaters were welcomed, spreading the love of skateboarding was the only intent.

The downhill skate event took place on Andrews Street. It was located on the West side of Letitbe's town. The bottom of the street led to the ice cream shop, that's where the crowd hung out around.

People from all over came by to watch the skaters skate. And there were tons of them; they came by at a great rate.

50/50 set up a stand and a speaker; they were right next to the ice cream shop. You were given a free cone, right after your run; all you had to do was stop.

The skate event was all about fun and for the skaters to show off their style. Andrews Street was a decent run. Its length was about half a mile.

One, two, three at a time, the skaters took off at the top of the hill. Each pulling out, move after move—oh what a show and a thrill.

One skater shot down the hill straight; he did so with tremendous speed.

Another skater did big S turns; that's how he continued to proceed.

Another skater took the hill backwards, she managed to make it all the way down.

Another skater went down the hill sitting. Crashing into 50/50's stand, he felt like a clown.

Young Agent – Whoa, buddy, I hope you're alright!

The skater yelled, 'All good!' as he stood upright.

The young agent was shocked that the boy crashed into 50/50's stand. 'Get this kid a cone,' he yelled, right into the mic he had in hand.

Bonez, Essie, Quigz, Sally, and the Goonsquad brothers all stood at the top of the hill. Getting ready to go, Sally stood there, remaining very still.

Bonez – Sally, it's great to see you. No pressure here, it's just for fun.

Sally – Yeah, say what you say, but believe me, you're not going to do better than this run.

Even though this event was for fun, Sally was determined to show off her skill. Her desire to leave the orphanage and rise to fame, she was determined again to fulfill.

Sally was wearing skater gloves, they had padding on the inside of the palm. With the Goonsquad brothers lined up next to her, Sally felt very calm.

Quickly taking off down the hill, Sally didn't seem to have any fear.

'Let's go, Sally!' Quigz yelled, as he seemed to be performing a cheer.

Essie looked over at Quigz; he was yelling and kicking his feet in the air. Essie yelled, 'Stop being a nerd, Quigz!' But Quigz continued without a care.

The Goonsquad brothers did a beeline; one after the other they followed on the right side. Sally picked up short bursts of speed, leaning back on her hand she was able to slide.

Quigz – Wow, I can't believe it. I've never seen anyone slide on their hand like that before!

Essie – Alright, Quigz, let's go me and you. Try to avoid hitting the floor.

Essie and Quigz took off, the crowd was cheering as Sally and the Goonsquad reached the bottom. Essie was squatting low and sliding, Quigz was skating but seemed to have forgotten.

Watching Sally and the Goonsquad celebrating as they were welcomed with loud cheers. Quigz was happy for Sally; he almost let out a few tears.

Essie's typical move was the slide; he always did them in short spurts. Just as he was finishing a long slide, his direction he quickly diverts.

Quigz, aimlessly cruising down the middle of the street, he gets right in Essie's way. Essie slides past him, just tipping his skateboard, Quigz then started to sway.

Quigz swayed towards the sidewalk and collided right into it. On the grass he thought to dive on his stomach, and he did so full commit. About thirty yards, it looked like Quigz slid. Looking back, Essie thought, 'What's wrong with this kid?'

Young Agent – Wow, what a thrill, Quigz, I hope you're alright! And Essie, nice skating, those slides are real tight! Folks, thanks for coming to 50/50's downhill skate event! And now it's time for our top skater, Bonez. Let's see what he has to present!

Bonez stood at the top of the hill. He cleared his mind and got very focused. His skateboard and the street in front of him were the only things that he noticed.

Bonez took off quickly, he headed straight down the hill. He got himself into a wheelie and showed off his impressive skill. First, he was on his back wheels; his front were raised in the air. Then he switched to the nose of the board, seamlessly, without a care.

As he reached the bottom of the hill, the crowd burst out into a cheer. Bonez was the best skater in town, and it seemed very clear.

Young Agent – What a show, I wouldn't have expected anything less! And now its time for a new skater— with her new moves, let's see if she can impress!

*"Not everything in life needs to be serious, there's always room for some fun.*

*Plus having fun opens our imagination, then solving problems is easily done."*

# CHAPTER 21 – THE NEW SKATER GIRL

Young Agent – Let me introduce you all to our new skater, Nicki from the top of town. She got tired of skating flat and started taking the streets down!

Nicki was the best step longboarder, over at the top of the hill. She was becoming tired of her usual flat ground skating, and needed a new thrill. So, she started skating Letitbe's hills and was seen by the young agent on his way home from work. Seeing Nicki's smooth longboarding moves made the young agent grin and smirk.

Standing at the top of Andrews Street, Nicki took a deep breath and thought about her run.

Nicki – I can step left foot over right, there and there, oh this should be some fun!

At the top of Letitbe the land was flat; there wasn't much downhill skateboarding to do. So, all the kids step long-boarded, and how this looks I will walk you through.

On a flat surface you cruise on your longboard and pick up a bit of speed. Walking end to end on the skateboard is how you would proceed.

Step longboarding was a dance. You step foot over foot and sometimes would spin. Now we look over towards Nicki; it was time for her run to begin.

Nicki takes off down the hill and perfectly lands the moves she planned to do. At one point, she carved with her legs crossed; for the town of Letitbe, these tricks were new.

Right before she reached the bottom, Nicki spun and had her back to the crowd. Everyone was going crazy, while cheering very loud. She was heading for 50/50's stand backwards, while moving with tremendous speed. She slid sideways and stopped herself smoothly. It was pretty impressive, yes indeed.

Young Agent – Ladies and Gentlemen, let's hear it for Nicki! She's the newest member on our team! Now Nicki, say a few words for the people.

Nicki – This all feels like a dream!

Nicki was a tall rocker girl. She had dark hair with a streak of purple. She wore fishnets on her arms and legs and had a shirt with a rocker turtle.

Nicki stood on 50/50's stand as she said a few words to the crowd. Watching the reactions of everyone, the young agent stood there, proud.

Young Agent – People, people, thank you all for the hospitality. All the money raised today, is going to a charity. Bonez, hop up there, stand next to Nicki, and let's get a photo. It's the skeleton boy and the rocker turtle, gotta love that new logo!

Bonez and Nicki stood on the stand, both smiling ear to ear. Going crazy for the both of them, 'Let's go, Bonez. Let's go, Nicki,' the crowd started to cheer.

Bree – Ugh, taking these photos really makes me sick.

Peep – Yeah, whatever, just take them quick.

Peep and Bree were deep in the crowd. Bree was around to take photos of the downhill skate event.

Bree – Don't worry, Peep. It's his loss, not yours. Plus working on yourself is time better spent.

Peep – Yeah, I know. I've just been painting a lot and working on my style. But I can't lie, it gets lonely sometimes. I haven't talked to anyone in quite a while.

Bree – Yeah, well, what's meant to be will always be, that's without a doubt. And let's talk about this all gray outfit, what's that all about?

Peep – I don't know, just haven't been feeling like me.

Bree – You have to get Bonez out of your head; believe me, that's the key.

Bonez by: Mr. Roses

Peep – I guess you're right. Gus seems to be caught up in the fame. I mean, I'm happy for him. Just wish things between me and him were the same.

Bree continued motivating Peep, saying how she needs to get back to herself and start dressing in her normal style.

Bree – Focus on what makes you happy, Peep. I want to see that bright smile.

Peep, smiling back, asked 'So how are things going with Essie and you?'

Bree – Just taking a break to focus on myself, but I know it's something we'll get through.

This entire conversation, Bree had been doing her usual thing, scouting the area with her camera, and taking photos of everything. Then in a moment, she felt everything in her body drain. This bad feeling in her stomach, it was hard for her to explain. Through the lens of the camera, she had seen an awful sight. Essie was taking down another girl's number; Bree's face turned all white.

Noticing this change in Bree's energy, Peep asked, 'Bree, are you alright?' Bree answered in a quiet tone, 'I can't believe my sight'. Then in the split of a second, things changed real quick.

Bree – I'm going to kill him, I'm going to kill him, Essie's talking to another chick!

With great speed, and in the heat of anger, Bree headed over toward the two.

Bree – I asked for a break so I can focus on myself, and this is what you go do!

Caught off guard, Essie fumbled on what to say.

Essie – This isn't what I wanted; this is because you got your way.

Bree – I said I just wanted some time, where we're not talking non-stop. So, you go out and talk to other girls, and our relationship you just drop?

Essie – I don't understand, what else should I be doing?

Bree – How about working on that cooking dream that I thought you were pursuing?

Bree headed back towards Peep, walking away with smoke coming out of her ears. 'Let's get out of here!' Bree shouted to Peep, as she held back a few tears.

Essie stood there alone as he thought about what Bree had said. 'Focus on myself, and work on my dream,' he couldn't get those words out of his head.

Quigz was with Sally and the Goonsquad brothers, they were celebrating a successful day. Bonez was hanging out on the stand with Nicki. Much change happened because of today.

*"There are many different types of fish deep out in the sea.*

*Find the one that makes you genuinely happy, believe me that's the key.*

*Until you find the one, be sure to keep working on you.*

*Your future life depends on today and everything you decide to do."*

141

# Chapter 22 – The Rest of the School Year

The rest of the school year, things between the crew broke apart. Bree was still out taking photos, Peep was working on her art. Peep would lock herself in her room, she would listen to music, and paint away. The more she worked on her art and herself, the less her clothes were gray.

Essie was only focusing on cooking. He was reading many, many books. He was experimenting with some recipes that he learned from famous cooks. He was working on this new dish, well, actually it was something you held in your hand. He was trying to think of food for skate events, while figuring out his own brand.

Quigz was always with Sally, still messing with her and the Goonsquad brothers since they were back at school. A boost in Sally's confidence and drive, that's what the successful skate event helped fuel.

Quigz latest prank involved a whoopee cushion; he slipped it in Sally's backpack when she didn't notice. It was at the bottom of the bag, under her books. And where she put the bag down was a bonus.

Sally walked into a crowded gymnasium, but there was barely any sound. She took her bag off, and went to sit, while dropping her bag on the ground.

The fart noise that the whoopee cushion made was loud. All eyes were on Sally from everyone in the crowd. Her face turned red as she started to blush. The nervous energy in her body started to rush.

Then she looked over at Quigz. He was right near her, laughing on the floor. Smiling, Sally headed towards him, and it seemed like a beating for Quigz was in store.

Bonez and Nicki hung out daily, they were constantly in the starlight. With all the attention she was starting to get, Nicki's skating career seemed very bright.

Now on Bonez's billboard, it had his face but Nicki's was there as well. Nicki even had her own rocker turtle gear, and it quickly started to sell.

As time went by, Bonez looked around and noticed a new trend. Rocker turtle stickers were everywhere, and many people were trying to be Nicki's friend.

The more Bonez and Nicki hung out while skating, the more recognized and famous Nicki became. Her friend requests on social media were out the door, while Bonez's declined as he slipped out of fame.

*"Always through life be ready, because problems will eventually come about.*

*When the sun shines for too long and too brightly, soon you may see a drought.*

*Now those around who truly care for you, will always help bear the storm.*

*Just keep moving through it day by day and at the end you will transform."*

# Chapter 23 - The First Few Weeks of Summer

The school year finally ended, and it was time for summer to start. The crew was involved with much action, but the crew was still apart.

Bree was still on the road. Since school ended, and the two made up, Essie joined along. He was selling his unique calzones at the skate events, and his sales turned out to be very strong.

After reading many cookbooks, one seemed to catch Essie's eye. *Delizioso* was the one, written by some random Italian guy.

Essie's invention was Not Your Average Calzone, it was something pretty unique. A standard calzone is stuffed with cheese and ham, wrapped in dough is the original technique.

Essie put a twist to it, instead of cheese and ham he decided to put a full meal. Anything you could eat on a plate was inside the calzone, and he did it all for a great deal.

Quigz pretty much every day would hang with Sally, either by the ice cream shop or when skating the streets. He was helping Sally get ready for Letitbe's End of Summer Race, and day after day this repeats.

Peep was still working on her art, and it seemed like she was building some traction. She was trying to sell her moon paintings, and they were finally seeing some action.

Bonez was entering a weird space, where he didn't feel like he was the top skater. Everyone seemed to love Nicki; the attention she got was always greater.

Nicki was skating the skate park, so Bonez decided to go skate 50/50's main shop. It was located up the hill near the orphanage, but not as close to the top.

The shop just had a few ramps; Bonez wanted to skate and clear his mind. Then all of a sudden, he turned his head as he heard 'Hey, Bonez' coming from behind.

Young Agent – Hey, Bonez, nice to see you. I'm glad you stopped in today. If you have a minute, let's chat; I have a few things I wanted to say.

Bonez by: Mr. Roses

Bonez – Yeah, sure, what's up, is everything alright?

Young Agent – Yeah, were doing great. The company's future seems very bright! I just wanted to talk to you about a small change we have to make. You being on the billboard is going to have to take a break.

Bonez – What?!? What do you mean? You want to take my picture down?

The young agent shrugged his shoulders, and on his face he had a frown.

Young Agent – Yes, unfortunately, but it's just business. Nicki is crushing it in the sales. There's always excitement around a new skater; I could explain to you all the details.

Bonez – No, it's alright, save it. You said it clear as day. Nicki's the new top skater, and I'm kicked to the curb. What else is there to say?

Young Agent – Hey, Bonez, don't be like that. You're still a great skater on our team.

Bonez – Yeah, but being the number two skater is not part of my dream.

Young Agent – Not to worry, Bonez, you can make it up at Letitbe's End of Summer Downhill Race. You're sure to be back on top again, all you have to do is win first place.

Bonez was motivated by the young agent's words, he said 'Thanks' as he headed out the door. Still a feeling of emptiness inside, Bonez thought he'd skate around and explore.

*"During the dark times of life, all the bad things seem to happen at once.*

*And if you don't catch yourself quickly, you could be stuck there for many months.*

*So just remember what is said, not all things last forever.*

*Focus on the lessons to be learnt and then work till things get better."*

# Chapter 23 - The First Few Weeks of Summer

Bonez by: Mr. Roses

# Chapter 24 – The Night of the New Moon

Bonez skated around Letitbe's streets as it started to get late. Trying to clear his mind, he could only think to skate.

He thought about his relationship with his friends. He thought about his travel through fame. He thought about the girl he lost. He felt sadness when he thought of her name.

He skated and skated up and down Letitbe's hills. There was a cool breeze, and it gave Bonez the chills.

As it got later and later, Bonez noticed it becoming quite dark. A travel to Kent Street's view, he thought he would embark.

Bonez stood at the top of the stairs, he looked down the middle of Kent Street's S design.

Bonez – I just need to win this race, and then the fame will again be mine.

Kent Street is the spot of Letitbe's End of Summer Race. Bonez was determined to again take first place. It's the quickest hill in all of their town. The view at the top was the best around: the ocean, the cliffs, and the cool breeze. A feeling of calm the view always guarantees.

Bonez sat on a rock and looked out to the ocean. He cleared his mind while looking at the waves in motion. He noticed that there was no moon reflecting off of the water. And then the thought came again, that he had lost her.

Bonez – What's wrong with me, how could I have been so blinded? I should have listened to my parents and made sure to be reminded. Mom said to trust my heart in whatever I try to pursue. And when I saw Peep in that gray outfit looking sad, what did I go do?

Bonez thought back to that day at lunch, when he noticed Peep in all gray. He felt he should have asked her if she's alright, but not a word he had to say.

Ignoring his heart and listening to the popular girl's call, Bonez seemed to have made the wrong decision. What he should have said to Peep in that moment, he now started to envision.

Then he thought back to what Poppa Bonez had said, 'They're not all really your friends, although most of them will act like it until the excitement finally ends.'

Now he thought back to recess, when Peep finally showed him her art.

Bonez - I felt again what we once had, deep down in my heart. And again, I made the mistake of taking the wrong side. When the popular girl found out my name, to Peep I rudely replied.

Bonez was realizing the poor decisions that he made because of the fame.

Bonez – I don't know who I was; I really wasn't the same.

Fame is just fame, it comes and it goes. What's important in life is the friends and family that you keep close. Essie's on the road with Bree, and Quigz is with Sally doing their own thing. Peep is off working on her art, loneliness for Bonez the fame seemed to bring.

For the rest of the night Bonez reflected on the past year and was determined to achieve a fresh start. He decided no matter what happens, going forward, he would only listen to his heart.

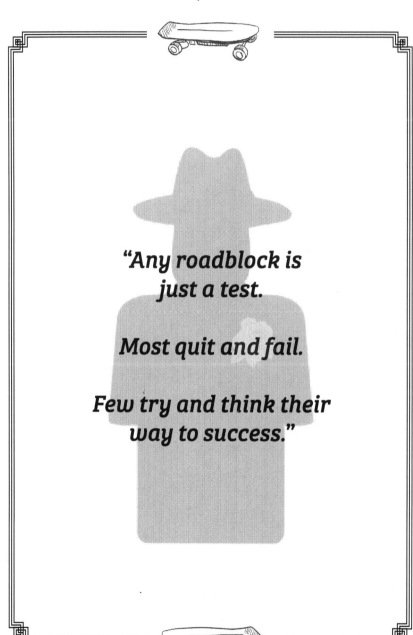

*"Any roadblock is just a test.*

*Most quit and fail.*

*Few try and think their way to success."*

# Chapter 24 - The Night of the New Moon

# Chapter 25 - Morning After a Long Night of Thinking

It was the morning after a long night, filled with much thought and reflection. It was now time for Bonez to try a brand-new direction.

Bonez – Last night the moon was dark, but I know there will be brighter days. I just need to be patient, work on myself and see how life plays.

Bonez headed over to the kitchen. Momma Bonez and Poppa Bonez were already there.

Momma Bonez – Morning Gus, are you hungry? Is there anything you'd like me to prepare?

Bonez – Hey, morning Mom. No, just some orange juice for me today.

Poppa Bonez – Hmm, you're not hungry, is everything ok?

Momma Bonez was by the counter. Poppa Bonez was sitting at the table with a paper in hand. They both were now looking at Bonez, and his body language they both scanned.

Bonez sat at the end of the table, with his orange juice that he swirled in a cup. He thought about what he wanted to say, and then he finally looked up.

Bonez – Yeah, just been thinking a lot. Things have been changing in the other direction. Maybe I haven't been focusing on what's important and need to make a correction.

Poppa Bonez – Let me guess, the rocker turtle girl. I've seen her here and there in the paper. There will always be something new and exciting, that's life's basic nature. So,

Bonez by: Mr. Roses

don't get yourself down when the excitement of life goes away. Only you can get yourself up when life starts feeling all gray.

Bonez – Yeah, I guess Nicki's part of it; since she came around my fame has slipped away. But I'm more concerned about my relationship with my friends—I hope it's all ok.

Poppa Bonez – I don't understand Gus, what do you mean?

Bonez – I was getting lost and caught up all in the fame scene. I was hanging with Nicki more, and all my friends drifted away.

Sadness and shame on his face, Bonez started to display.

Momma Bonez – Honey, don't feel down. Anything in life can be fixed. Only death can't be changed.

On the top of his head, she kissed.

Poppa Bonez – Your mother's right Gus. Real friends will always come back around. And if they don't, then they weren't real friends.

Poppa Bonez said as he frowned.

Chapter 25 - Morning After a Long Night of Thinking

Momma Bonez – So where have Essie and Quigz been? You haven't mentioned their names in a while. How's Quigz with the crazy red hair, and how's Essie with that famous smile?

Bonez – They're both doing good. Each have been doing things on their own. Essie's on the road with this girl Bree, and he made his own calzone. Quigz has been hanging with this girl Sally and training her for Letitbe's end of summer skate event.

Momma Bonez – Wow, I'm glad to hear. Sounds like time well spent! And what about that girl from last summer? I remember you being on the phone with her almost every night.

Bonez – Peep, yeah because of the fame, things between me and her haven't been right. I spent most of my time with the popular girls; with Peep I barely hung out. Now I'm sure she's just been painting; her missing me I highly doubt.

After hearing Bonez's words, something clicked in Poppa Bonez's mind. He started scanning through the paper, there was something he was trying to find.

Poppa Bonez – Hey, Gus, what was this girl's name?

'Her name is Peep,' Bonez said with a bit of shame.

Poppa Bonez – Here in the paper, it says there's a girl Peep having an art show in that little art store. Maybe you should go check it out. It says it opens today at four oh four.

Bonez felt a rush of energy through his body, it lifted him right out of his seat. 'I need to make up with her and here's my chance,' in his mind he began to repeat.

Bonez decided to eat breakfast, as his appetite finally appeared. The gloomy feeling of being down and regretful, for now seemed to have disappeared.

For the rest of the day Bonez cleared his mind. He thought about Peep and the things he wanted to say. A new focus into what's important in life, Bonez now started to display.

*"Through the middle of a storm, clouds could block sight of the land.*

*Trapped on a boat in the middle of the ocean, the storm may seem to command.*

*We must be patient and have faith that eventually we will find the way on our quest.*

*Through patience, hard work and reflection we are sure to find land and sure to be gracefully blessed."*

Bonez by: Mr. Roses

# CHAPTER 26 - PEEP'S ART SHOW

It was getting close to four oh four, that's when Peep's art show was planned to start. The thought of seeing Peep today warmed Bonez's heart.

Bonez headed out of his house and skated down to the show. The art store was down by the ice cream shop, where the two first met a long while ago. It was a round building painted white, and inside it had a black floor. Bonez hopped off his skateboard and paused for a second, then walked towards the front door.

Through the glass door, he saw a crowd and walked in with a bit of hesitation. He stood in the back and saw Peep in the front, giving a quick presentation.

Peep – Thank you all for coming; this has been such an honor. And thank you to the art store for being an incredible sponsor. These paintings are all about the phases of the moon. They show the different stages of life from day to day. Some days are dark, and some are in-between, but the moon's surely bright today!

Everyone spoke highly about Peep's paintings as the night continued and progressed. With tons of smiles, and dressed in all bright colors, great joy Peep expressed.

Bonez then saw an opportunity as the crowd started to disperse. Peep was just talking with Bree, so he thought he'd walk over and converse.

Bree – Hey, hold up, I think you mean to walk in the other direction.

Bree immediately dismissed Bonez. Her intent was for Peep's protection.

Bonez – Hey guys, I'm not looking for any trouble. I just want to say, Peep, your art's really great.

Bree – Awesome, now the door's right behind you, Bonez. Just turn around and keep walking straight.

Bonez looked at Peep, he had sadness in his eyes. Quietly Peep just stood there, it caught Bonez by surprise.

With Peep standing there emotionless, and Bree looking ready for a fight. Bonez turned around and walked away; it was what he thought was right.

Peep – I feel bad. I can't just let him walk away all crushed.

Peep stood there feeling anxious—her hair she nervously brushed.

Bree – Forget about him. He gets what he deserves.

Peep – I don't know. I'm going to talk to him and just have a few words.

As Bonez was about to hop on his skateboard, Peep walked out the door and said, 'Hey Gus wait!' Bonez turned around while smiling; he knew this ending wasn't their fate.

Bonez – Hey, Peep, I'm glad to see you. Your art really is amazing.

Peep – Thanks, Gus, I appreciate it, but I don't need all the praising. You obviously came here for a reason, so what do you have to say?

Seriousness and focus on her face, Peep seemed to display.

With butterflies in his stomach, Bonez said, 'I guess I just miss hanging out with you. I wasn't myself for the past year, and I'm sorry for anything I put you through.'

Finally, there was a change in Peep's expression as she started to feel warmth in her heart.

Peep – You know you really did hurt me, but because of you I found my art.

Happy for Peep, but still slightly ashamed, Bonez had a slanted smile on his face. A perfect ending would be Bonez and Peep getting back together, but unfortunately this wasn't the case.

Peep still missed Bonez. She always knew he was good at heart. She was waiting for the excitement to end, so they could give it a fresh start. In the meantime, she was painting and now is getting big with her art. She has a scheduled tour for the rest of summer, and tomorrow it's planned to start.

Peep – Gus, thanks for the apologies, but I need to go and follow this art tour. I have to focus on myself and my work, and success I think I'll secure.

Disappointed but understanding, Bonez looked down at the floor. Looking up and smiling he said, 'You're going to do great, that's for sure.'

After a hug, the two split apart, each in their own direction. Although still apart, Bonez and Peep, again, both felt a connection.

Alone through the summer, Bonez spent most of his days. His fame had quieted, but randomly he'd still see a fan and get some praise. Mostly, each day, Bonez would just be thinking and skating to clear his mind. He needed something to lift him—an idea he needed to find.

Then finally an idea had hit him. Through his body excitement raced in and out! He knew all he had to do was win Letitbe's End of Summer Race, and I'll tell you what that's all about.

Bonez missed hanging out with Peep, that's something that he knew. But now she was out on this art tour, so what could he do? He thought, 'If I win this race, the young agent said the fame would come back again. Once I have the fame, then maybe, just maybe, I can tour other skate competitions then?'

Bonez - With the fame I should grow on social media, and everyone will again know my name. And maybe if I do my own thing and line up a skate tour with Peep's art tour, things between us could be the same.

The rest of the summer Bonez focused on skating, he was prepping for Letitbe's End of Summer Downhill Race. Committed to making his ideas a reality, he was determined to take first place.

*"It starts with a hunch, then a feeling of excitement. A new idea can give a feeling of enticement.*

*But how could we know if this idea's truly the right thing to do? Nobody could see the future; nobody has that view.*

*It's about how the idea makes us feel, our gut will never lie. If it makes us happy and excited, it's worth giving the idea a try."*

171

# CHAPTER 27 - LETITBE S END OF SUMMER DOWNHILL RACE

At the end of a lonely summer, we finally come to the big race. Bonez believed he was following his heart and felt in a calm place. When he thought of his plan—to secure fame and go out solo on a skate tour. The excited energy in his stomach made him confident, the win he was sure to secure.

At the top of Kent Street, it was the start of Letitbe's End of Summer Downhill Race. It was a race down to the beach Seaview, and it moved at a quick pace. It was a bit of a cloudy day, which made it tough to skate this S-shaped street. Bonez just arrived at the top, and there were a few familiar faces to greet.

Letitbe's End of Summer Downhill Race, was the town's event but 50/50 was there to support the team. Young agent was talking with Bonez, then as Nicki arrived, the crowd started to scream.

Bonez saw Essie and Bree there. They were both lost in their own world. Bree was zipping around taking photos. Essie was making calzones that he stuffed and he curled.

Bonez also saw Quigz and Sally, oh and the Goonsquad brothers I can't forget to mention. But there was one face he hoped to find as he scanned the crowd with much attention.

Nowhere in the crowd was Peep's bright smile. Bonez hoped to see her; it's been quite a while.

Announcer – Attention all, attention loud, may I have the attention of the skaters and the crowd? Thank you all for coming to Letitbe's End of Summer Downhill Race! If you're ready then so am I. Let's see who out of these three takes first place!

The first to line up was Nicki, she had her rocker turtle shirt and had her step longboard in her hand. Next was Sally dressed in all yellow, from head to toe her huge skateboard spanned.

Lastly, Bonez lined up. He had his little banana board and was wearing the skeleton boy shirt. He was calm, focused, and confident, while remaining very alert.

The crowd was yelling loud and cheering, most were chanting Nicki's name. Bonez blocked out the sound, as he thought about his goal: winning this race and securing the fame.

Bonez by: Mr. Roses

Announcer – People, people, guess what time it is? I think you all know. Skaters, pay attention! Three, two, one—now take off and go!!!

Bonez, Sally, and Nicki took off skating as the crowd started heading down the stairs. Nicki was leading as they approached the first turn, with great speed she didn't have any cares.

Because of the clouds today, it wasn't the easiest task to see far ahead of you down the street. Sand in the middle of the road, gave Nicki and the floor a chance to meet.

Seeing Nicki fall around the turn, from the line of sand crossing the entire street, Bonez squatted low and jumped in the air—a perfect ollie he was able to complete.

Landing perfectly on the other side, Bonez turned and looked to Sally falling back on her hand.

Bonez – All my competition's down and out. This race couldn't have been better planned.

Swiftly, Bonez was approaching the first stair landing. He was relaxed with his hands in the air. He looked at the crowd and popped a wheelie, then did another ollie and spun around without a care.

Now facing backwards, he couldn't believe his eyes. Sally was flying right past him, it caught Bonez by surprise. He noticed now what Sally was wearing, she had one on each of her hands. 'She didn't fall, she was sliding with those gloves,' Bonez now understands.

Spinning around and kicking quickly, Bonez pushed off the floor as Sally approached the next turn. Sliding on her hand quick and smoothly, redemption Sally seemed to yearn.

Bonez rounded the turn as quick as he could, then started kicking fast down the last incline. But it wasn't enough to beat Sally. Upset, he watched her cross the finish line.

At the bottom of the stairs, in the parking lot by Seaview, everyone was congratulating Sally on her exciting win. Quigz lifted Sally in the air with the Goonsquad brothers, while defeat and sadness Bonez felt within.

Bonez – Maybe I'm not supposed to be famous, and maybe I'm not supposed to be with Peep.

He didn't really care about the fame, but his care for Peep was deep.

Bonez – No, it's alright. I know for me and Peep it's meant to be. Dad always says life finds a way to work itself out, the path right now I just can't see.

Deep in reflection, Bonez thought about Peep and the time that they spent together. He thought about the date at the ice cream shop and how, compared to the fame, hanging out with her was better.

Bonez by: Mr. Roses

Feeling down and lonely, he watched the crowd as they celebrated Sally's exciting win. Then a familiar hug, came from behind, and happiness Bonez felt within.

*"Sometimes our plans don't work out the way we thought they would.*

*Sometimes we end up better off through ways we could have never understood.*

*What's important is having the faith that we will eventually find our way.*

*And if we fail, that's alright. Tomorrow's always another day."*

# Chapter 28 - Closing

After Letitbe's End of Summer Downhill Race, things seemed to have changed in a new direction. The crew was out, doing their own thing, but this time they were all in connection.

Bree was off following the skate scene, still taking photos at every skate event. And now Essie was also following the skate scene in an R.V. with his parents, his calzones were what paid the rent. He was on many magazine covers; he had them all saved and stacked in a pile. Always showing off a different calzone, but always having the same smile.

After her win at the race, young agent asked Sally if she would accept 50/50 being her sponsor. She smiled with tears in her eyes, saying, 'Yes it would be my honor.'

Now with three skaters finally on their team, 50/50 can enter into all professional competitions. Bonez, Sally, and Nicki traveled all over, and 50/50 took care of all the commissions.

The Goonsquad brothers were inspired by Sally and vowed to continue school at her request. 'Focus on school and find your dream,' these were the words Sally stressed.

Peep was still touring around for her art and was able to line it up with the skate scene. Now at every competition the crew traveled together. It was something that felt like a dream.

Last but not least, we have Quigz—he too traveled with the crew since 50/50 sponsored him as well. Sally's logo ended up being a yellow chicken. Quigz was sponsored to be her mascot, and much merchandise he helped sell.

Life is always filled with ups and downs as each person goes through their days. It's all about how you respond to a situation, and everybody has different ways.

## Chapter 28 - Closing

There're two things to always remember, the first is to always follow your heart. The second is that each day is new and always perfect for a fresh start.

After a lonely summer, Bonez again had it all. He was killing it at the skate competitions and again was standing tall. But none of that really mattered to him because he knew he had the real prize. It was Peep right there standing next to him. Happiness was looking in her eyes.

*"The search for purpose and meaning in life is everyone's true goal.*

*To find the thing to do with our time that makes us happy deep down to our soul.*

*It's a journey that goes on for forever, so be sure to enjoy the ride.*

*And if your lucky you'll meet the one, who wants to take the journey of life with you together by your side."*

# Chapter 28 - Closing

# BONUS ACTIVITIES

**Mr. Roses has a few questions for you, find the right answer and master the review.**
(Read each question and circle the correct answer.)

1.) **Who** in this story is chasing their dreams?

A.) Bonez
B.) Sally
C.) Essie
D.) All the above

2.) **What** was Bonez original goal at the beginning of the story?

A.) To be famous
B.) To become rich
C.) To be the best skater around
D.) To become the Skeleton Boy

3.) **Where** does Bonez and Peep meet?

A.) In Hawaii
B.) At the Skatepark
C.) Outside the Ice Cream Shop
D.) At School

4.) **Why** does Bonez start to ignore Peep?

A.) Because he lost his memory and forgot who she is
B.) Because he signed a contract to be sponsored by 50/50
C.) Because he became caught up in the fame
D.) Because Peep left and moved to Italy

5.) **When** does Bonez realize he messed up?

A.) When Nicki comes to town and joins 50/50
B.) After reflecting on the past year the night at Kent Street
C.) When he is in his room talking to Peep
D.) When Quigz hit him in the head with the acorn

6.) **How** does Bonez fix things?

A.) He accepts his past actions and decides to follow his heart going forward
B.) He puts together a new video showing off his moves
C.) He meets Peep and convinces her to take him back
D.) He decides to move away

## Mr. Roses Word Search Puzzle.
### (Search for the words listed below.)

```
R P P A T K Z K L Q S A B T E
C C T B S S E C C U S G Z E H
Y O D R E A M E T I Q G R C U
G V N K W N F K R U I B E M D
V S A S V O G K H U M B L E X
D I A A I I E I Q F L F H M D
T W F W G S P G U E F I V M L
D R P D S K T M Z W G W A X E
X W O I Y· E P E E P C F A F R
A Q E F S R N M N V P A A C G
Z S T P F O Q C Z C A J X K I
F C A B B E L W R Q Y E L Z U
E J K R G B X S G I J T J K Q
L X S A L L Y J S V L S L N K
U T K E S I W H G Q B B X Z E
```

1.) Bonez  2.) Essie  3.) Quigz  4.) Peep

5.) Bree  6.) Sally  7.) Dream  8.) Effort

9.) Consistency  10.) Failure  11.) Success

12.) Humble

There are many lessons to be learnt from this story but there are three specific ones I want to go through here. The first is about deciding on a dream for the future and the importance of this I want to make clear.

When you have an idea of what you want for the future, that idea will act as your north star. It will guide you on your journey ahead and ensure that you go very far.

It will be your point of reference that you can begin forming ideas around. When you put those ideas together, you can make a plan that looks quite sound.

Then with much, much effort, you can begin putting the plan into motion. You'll know you're on the right track when your life is filled with tons of great emotion.

**What is your dream for the future?**

_____

_____

_____

*Fill in your dream above*

190

Once you decide on your dream, set off planning away. Think of what you can do to make your dreams come true, and then start working today. The sooner you set off and get going, the sooner you can then fall down. Believe me, it will happen often, so learn to lose the frown.

_____

_____

_____

_____

_____

_____

_____

_____

_____

_____

*List out a few goals that you can begin working towards*

191

The second lesson I want to go through is about failure and what it really is. Failure isn't really that bad, it's just life's little quiz. Each failure is just a lesson that could teach us many things. Once we discover the lesson to be learnt, much joy and growth it brings.

As you're working towards your dreams, many roadblocks will block the road. Turn around, you'll never make it, these are some of the words you may be told.

But if you believe in your dream with your heart, and there isn't a doubt in your mind. Whatever roadblock presents itself, there will be another rout that you will find.

Each time you get a bit closer, each time you'll get knocked back down. This is the way life teaches us and show's us where happiness is found.

It's only through struggle and resistance that true growth is created. And appreciation for it all will come, but only after it has been long awaited.

So as you go along the road towards your dreams, it's critical to choose the right people to join along. Because when struggles finally present themselves, the people close to you will help you stay strong.

Some may be your family, and some may be your friends. Regardless of what happens along the journey, the real ones will be there when it all finally ends.

So the third and final lesson I want to point out here is to search for and cherish genuine relations. Whether it be family or business, with it, you will overcome all complications.

# Learn to Draw Bonez

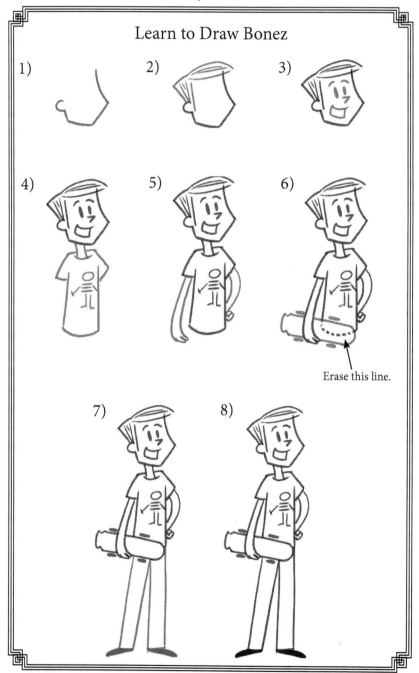

1)

2)

3)

4)

5)

6)

Erase this line.

7)

8)

# Learn to Draw Peep

Visit: HouseOfRoses.org to learn how to draw
the rest of the crew!

Answers:

1.) D 2.) C 3.) C 4.) C 5.) B 6.) A

## Reader:

"Thank you again for taking some time to read through this book. It has been a long and slow process bringing this book into existence. Thankfully its finally here and is something I believe will help guide the reader to great achievement and satisfaction in their life. There are more underlying and deeper lessons being taught throughout this book. For more advanced information on success and inspiration please visit my website:

- HouseOfRoses.org

If you have anything you want to ask me or if you want to share any of your own achievements, please contact me at:

- Mr.RosesEmail@Gmail.com

No matter what happens in our life and no matter what our current situation in life is, there are always ways to work things out. The key is to remain calm and think. Thought is the true gift that we all are born with. Thought has allowed humans to create everything that exists today.

If you are upset with your current life situation or if you simply desire more, start with thought. Think about what you would like your future life to look like. Then start thinking about what it would take to get there. Then think about what you could start doing today and start. Then with tons of patience and much hard work, your dreams will eventually be your reality."

- Mr. Roses

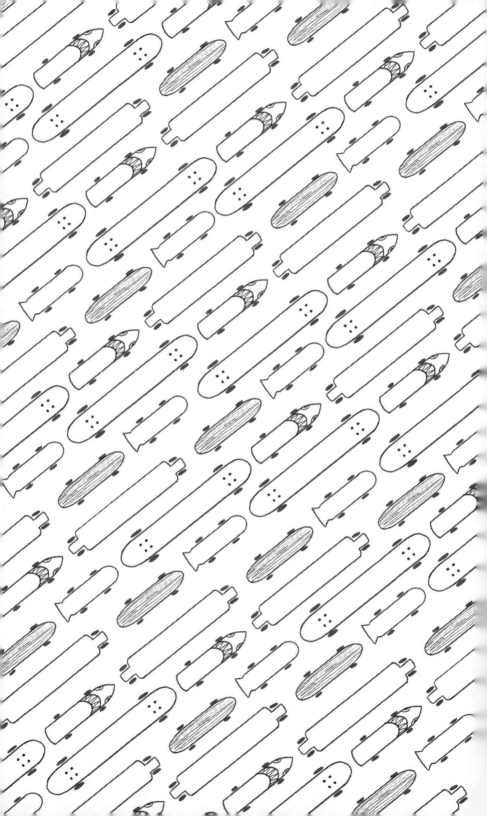

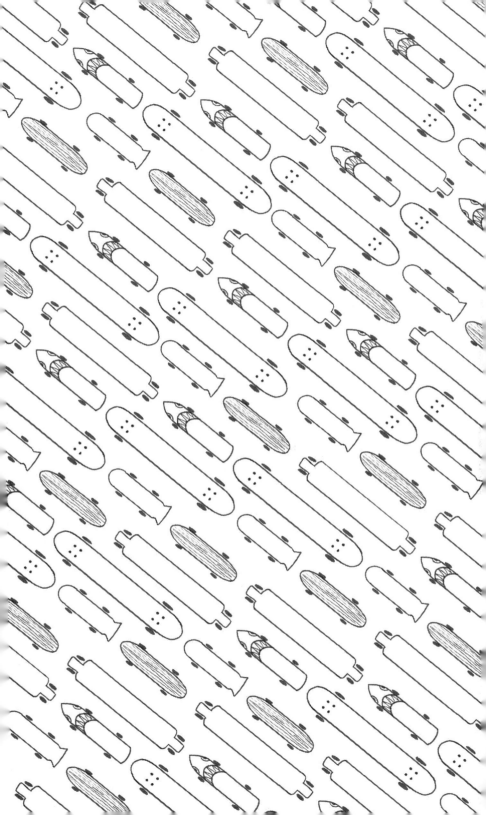

Made in the USA
Las Vegas, NV
22 August 2021